Is their cover blown?

She can't know, I told myself. *ATAC security is way too good. She can't have gotten past it.*

I completely believed that. In my head. In my stomach, I wasn't quite as sure.

Veronica raised her eyebrows. "Interesting choice," she told Georgina. "And something of a bargain, because Frank's secret gives away something about Joe as well."

My palms began to sweat. A secret that was about me and Joe? How many things could that be?

Strategy. I needed strategy. What should Joe and I do if we were outed right here and now?

Deny it? Say it was some ratings stunt of Veronica's? Or something she and the other producers had come up with to create tension in the house? I don't watch a lot—or actually any—reality TV, but Joe says they all end up having lots of fights among the contestants. That was definitely turning out to be true on our show.

Or should we admit to the truth and warn everybody that they were in danger? Just explain that Joe and I had been placed undercover as contestants because the death threats they'd received were being taken very seriously—and for good reason, since several people in this house had already been victims of murder!

THE HARDY BOYS

Undercover Brothers®

Available from Simon & Schuster

THE HARDY BOYS

Undercover Brothers®

FRANKLIN W. DIXON

#24 Murder House

Aladdin Paperbacks

New York   London   Toronto   Sydney

East

❧

ALADDIN PAPERBACKS
An imprint of Simon & Schuster Children's Publishing Division
1230 Avenue of the Americas, New York, NY 10020
Copyright © 2008 by Simon & Schuster, Inc.
All rights reserved, including the right of reproduction in whole or in part in any form.
ALADDIN PAPERBACKS, THE HARDY BOYS MYSTERY STORIES, HARDY BOYS UNDERCOVER BROTHERS, and related logo are registered trademarks of Simon & Schuster, Inc.
Designed by Sammy Yuen Jr.
The text of this book was set in Aldine 401 BT.
Manufactured in the United States of America
First Aladdin Paperbacks edition September 2008
10 9 8 7 6 5 4 3 2 1
Library of Congress Control Number 2008920166
ISBN-13: 978-1-4169-6409-4
ISBN-10: 1-4169-6409-6

TABLE OF CONTENTS

Sabotage

I figured the wheels of my Suzuki RM-Z450 had to be smoking as I wove through the orchard. But I didn't let up on the throttle. I had the lead, and I didn't want to lose it.

I broke out of the trees and into the field behind the tennis courts. Mounds of dirt were heaped up all across it. I could maneuver the bike around them. But I'd lose time.

The three mounds almost dead ahead weren't so much different from the triple jump at Highland Park. I'd taken that one lots of times.

Okay, this hill was a little higher, I decided as I started up it. I heard at least one bike coming up behind me. Fast. I moved into attack position.

Standing on the dirt bike's pegs. Knees tightened around the tank. My elbows up and out.

Yeah, this hill was definitely higher than the first of the triple back home. I kept an even throttle as I approached the top. Here it came. I was about to go airborne.

Stay low over the jump, I reminded myself. It would buy me a few extra seconds. Not much. But a few seconds could be the difference between winning and losing. I was undercover as a reality show contestant, and that meant I should want to win more than anything. Somebody on the show wanted to win so badly he or she had sent death threats to all of the contestants.

As my bike came off the top of the hill, I pushed down on the right footpeg and pulled up on the left side of the handlebars. The bike laid out flat. Nice. The move had stopped the upward motion of the jump. That's where I picked up the extra seconds.

I got on the throttle right before I hit ground to help the rear suspension take the impact of landing. Solid. Now I had to—

My strategy was worthless. A rider came over the hill behind me kamikaze style, lost control of their ride, and slammed into my back wheel.

We both went down. And another bike was just going airborne. There was no time to do anything but curl my body into a protective ball. I felt the bike's heat on the top of my head as it cleared me. Next time I might not be so lucky.

I scrambled to my feet and saw that it was Georgina who'd taken me out. "Come on, we've got to get out of the way before someone else takes the jump!"

I grabbed my bike by the handlebars, got it up, then ran it down the side of the hill, out of the path of the most direct route to the grocery shelves at the end of the field. That's what this race was. A contest to see who could get the groceries on their list back to the mansion first.

"Are you okay?" I asked Georgina.

She pulled off her helmet. "Yeah. But the bike's messed up," she answered.

"I don't know if mine got damaged or not," I said.

"No, I mean mine was messed up before. The brakes stopped working," Georgina told me. She slapped the seat of her bright purple Kawasaki.

The dirt bikes we were using for the race were brand-new. That could mean only one thing.

Sabotage.

Everybody Has Secrets

"Everyone, everyone! Please gather round," Veronica called from her spot on the patio near the large fountain. She backed up a step as we headed toward her. I'm sure she was afraid we'd contaminate her. We were all sweaty and dirt smeared and grass stained.

Veronica was perfumed and nail painted and color coordinated in her pale blue suit and pale blue spike heels. She should have looked like TV Host Barbie in all that perfect, with her white-blond hair smoothed back into one of those knot things that aren't buns but that I don't have the words to actually describe, having only one X chromosome.

But the smile she gave the group was pure, lipstick-coated nastiness. You'd never see Barbie looking so *eeevil*. And enjoying it so much.

"First, I want to announce the winner of this competition." She paused. Of course. When *Deprivation House* actually aired, there would probably be a commercial break right here. "Brynn Fulgham got her groceries home before the rest of you. That means she will be deciding the next deprivation."

"Don't take away toiletries!" Ripley called. Ripley Lansing was the group's celebrity, although she was only famous for having famous—and rich— parents. "The boys smell bad enough now that they hardly ever shower. We won't survive if they lose deodorant privileges!"

"Who can shower when there's no hot water anymore?" Gail protested. Gail's parents definitely weren't rich. So not rich they didn't always have enough money to pay the heating bill. Sometimes Gail had to go to bed in her coat to stay warm.

"All the girls still shower," Ripley shot back.

"I don't care about deodorant or shampoo or any of that. I just want to be able to keep my drawing supplies," Hal said. Hal was always drawing plans for the planet around which he planned to design a computer game.

I tried to figure out what Joe Carr would want most. That was my cover. A rich boy from

Connecticut, adopted by a different family from my brother, Frank Dooley. It was hard to come up with anything. We'd already lost cell phones, iPods, junk food.

"Brynn, I'm begging you. Think of the odor," Ripley pleaded.

"Now, now. It's Brynn's decision," Veronica reminded everyone. "And she doesn't need to make it until tomorrow night. Right now, I want to take some time for us all to get to know one another a little better."

"I know these losers as well as I want to," James Sittenfeld told her. "I've been trapped in the house with them for almost a month."

We had been spending almost all our time together since our first day as contestants on *Deprivation House*, a reality show where teenagers saw how long they could last without luxury items. The network probably thought it would be fun for old folks to laugh at the younger generation freaking out because they were unable to go online, watch TV, text message, and talk on the cell at the same time.

Still, I wouldn't mind learning some more about the other kids in the house. They were all suspects. See, my brother and I weren't really contestants. That was just our cover. We were actually here on an assignment for American Teens Against Crime, an organization our dad helped found. ATAC puts teens undercover in places where adult operatives would stick out too much. Like on a reality show where all the contestants are kids. Get me?

Frank and I ended up here because all the contestants had received death threats. And since we'd shown up, a lot of nasty things had been happening. Some people had even died. None of them contestants. At least not yet.

So that's why I was up for finding out as much as possible about every kid in the house. Although I've got to say, if James wasn't a suspect and was just some guy, I'd be happy to never learn another thing about him. Like last night, I found out he clips his toenails—with his teeth. I already knew he was maniacally competitive, and a bully. But I'm not biased or anything. Detectives have to keep open minds. And I'm a detective. Just because James is your basic rat dropping in human form doesn't mean he's a killer.

"George and Georgina only joined us very recently, and I thought some of you might be curious as to why they were allowed to join our game so late," Veronica continued.

"To get ratings," Olivia muttered.

Veronica pretended not to hear her. "The truth is, I got a letter from their father asking me to consider allowing them to come to Deprivation House. It was so touching that the network and I just couldn't say no." She gave a sweet smile. And when she smiles like that, somebody's about to get sucker punched.

"Let me read it to you," Veronica went on. I did a face check on George and Georgina. Not happy. And not happy. I miscalculated. Make that two somebodys were going to get a Veronica smackdown. She began:

"Dear Ms. Wilmont, I saw a commercial for your upcoming show, *Deprivation House*, and I had to write to you. You and your house may be the last hope for my fifteen-year-old twins, George and Georgina. All their lives, their mother and I have given them everything they've asked for. As an example, for their last birthday, they received a trip to Maui with eight of their friends, Georgina received a Tennessee walking horse, and George an Escalade, in addition to thousands of dollars' worth of smaller presents.

"It would have been our pleasure to give our children these gifts. We want them to enjoy all life has to offer. But they don't seem to understand that not everyone has the privileges they do. They have no concept of the work that has gone into earning the money to pay for their lifestyle. They show no appreciation. They show almost no awareness that a horse or a car are any different from the air or the ground, something that is simply there at any time for their use.

"That's why I'm begging you to make them a part of your show. Not so they have a chance to win a million dollars. That would only make the situation more nauseating. All I want is for George and Georgina to have the opportunity to live without what they consider necessities, but what the majority of the population considers luxuries. For a brief time, I want them to be deprived. I know that this is not your responsibility. It is their mother's and mine. But we have not been able to take control of the situation, and that is why we are asking for your help. No, begging.

"I know the deadline to enter the contest has passed, but please don't refuse us. Please give George and Georgina a chance to become better people.

Sincerely,
George Taggart"

Veronica carefully refolded the letter. "Of course, I couldn't say no."

I did another George and Georgina face check. Very not happy. And very not happy. In fact, make that George red-faced, looking like he was about to go nuclear. And Georgina, face drained of color, looking like she was plotting somebody's long and painful death.

"If their parents don't want them to have the money, does that mean they're ineligible to win it?" Olivia asked.

I wasn't surprised that she was the first to get that question out. Olivia is the queen of strategy in the game.

"That would be completely uncool," George burst out. "If we're here, and we have to follow all the same rules as everybody here, we should have the same chance to win the cash as anybody else."

"George and Georgina will follow the same rules and have the same privileges as the rest of you," Veronica answered. "Including the chance to win the prize money."

"What would you even do with the cash?" Gail protested. "It sounds like you have two of everything that exists already." Gail was a latecomer to the House too, just not as late as the twins. She joined the group about a week and a half into the game as a surprise twist.

"Ever heard of legal emancipation?" Georgina

asked. Some of the color had returned to her cheeks, and her eyes were bright with excitement. "That's what I would do with the money. Hire myself a lawyer. Cut all ties with my parents. As you might have guessed, they're complete control freaks, emphasis on the freaks. And use the rest of the cash to live on."

"My plan exactly," said George.

"Not until you just heard me say it," Georgina snapped. "You never have any ideas of your own."

"It doesn't matter, because only one of us is winning the moola, and it's going to be me," George told his sister. "Don't think I'm sharing, either. I'll be living solo, and you'll be home with the freaks."

"You've never won anything without my help and you know it," Georgina shot back. "The only reason I didn't win today is that my bike was messed with. You couldn't—"

"Hey, don't fight," James cut in. He gave a smile every bit as nasty as Veronica's, but minus the lipstick. "It's pointless. Neither of you is going to win. 'Cause I'm winning. Everybody else here has already accepted it. You'll just have to suck it up too."

"Did you forget that Brynn won today's competition?" Olivia demanded.

"Competitions aren't everything," James reminded

her. "It's all about how you handle the deprivation. And I'm stone. Nothing gets to me."

"You practically meowed when your exercise equipment got—" Olivia began.

Veronica clapped her hands. "Enough of this bickering. It's very entertaining, but I think we've got plenty of footage. Now, I imagine it must have been somewhat humiliating for George and Georgina to have had that letter read aloud to all of you—and of course to all the viewers when our show airs. So I think it's only fair that a few other secrets are revealed today. George, why don't you pick one of the other contestants, and I'll reveal a secret about them."

"Why does he get to pick?" Georgina whined.

Veronica ignored her. Veronica is very good at ignoring anything that displeases her.

"What secrets are you even talking about, anyway?" demanded James.

Veronica ignored him, too.

I shot a fast glance at Frank. His face was carefully blank. But I knew we both had the same question James did. What secrets did Veronica know? She couldn't know the real reason Frank and I were here. Could she?

If she outed us, our mission was over. We wouldn't be able to protect anyone in the house if our cover was blown.

George glanced around the group, taking his time, enjoying making the rest of us sweat. What a guy. "I pick . . ." He did a dramatic pause. He'd learned something from Veronica. "Ripley."

Olivia snorted. "Don't we know all her secrets already?" she asked. "She's in the paper practically every day. Even though all she's famous for is going to parties and spending her parents' money."

Olivia really had a thing against rich people. It wasn't Ripley's fault that her dad *was* the drummer for Tubskull and her mom ran a cosmetics company and that they had a zillion dollars. I guess it was her fault that she'd been pretty obnoxious before she came to the house—stomping on paparazzi cameras, getting waiters fired for pretty much nothing, and other brat stuff like that. But she'd been cool since we'd met her.

"She saved my life," I reminded Olivia. "And Bobby T's." Bobby T was a contestant who had already been booted from the show.

"She saved your life and Bobby's so she wouldn't get her platinum American Express cut up by her parents," Olivia corrected me. "We all know that Ripley's mom and dad got sick of all the bad publicity she was getting, and that they told her she had to start proving she could be nice—and getting the good PR to prove it—or they wouldn't give her any more money. She'd have to wait until she was thirty, when she got her inheritance, before she saw another dollar."

"What if they did?" Ripley asked. The muscles in her neck tensed, but she forced a smile. I have to say, she was working pretty hard at the nice. "Is it so wrong for them to want me to be a better person? Isn't that what your parents are supposed to do?" She looked from George to Georgina. "It's what your dad was trying to do by getting you on the show, right?"

"Yeah, what a great guy," George answered with a sneer. "I really respect him."

"We're getting off the subject of Ripley's secret," said Veronica.

"Is the secret that Ripley is the one who put Joe and Bobby T in danger in the first place?" Olivia jumped in. "Because I think it's way too convenient that she was right on the spot when two people needed rescuing."

"Frank was the one who took a chainsaw to the sauna when people got trapped in there," Ripley protested. "Why aren't you accusing him of setting things up to look like a hero?"

"It was Mitch who rigged the sauna. It was Mitch who put peanut oil in Bobby T's toothpaste to give him the allergic reaction. He's the one who fed jimsonweed to the dog who attacked Joe too," I reminded everyone. Mitch was a bank robber who'd hidden cash in the house before he'd gone to prison. He was trying to get us all out of there so he could collect it.

"Do you really know that for sure?" asked Olivia. "Stuff kept happening."

"Mary is the one who was sabotaging us. You know that," Joe said. Mary was a former fellow contestant who'd confessed to most of the sabotage before the police took her away.

"She said she didn't put the glass shards in the ice," Olivia continued. "And she also denied setting that fire in Bobby's room, and putting the knives in Brynn's makeup bag. Why wouldn't she admit to those when she admitted to everything else? And there was that writing in the—"

"And somebody messed with my dirt bike," Georgina interrupted. "I was completely sabotaged."

"Yeah, right," said George. "She always has an excuse when she loses," he explained.

"I only lose when—" Georgina began.

"Enough!" Veronica ordered. "I can see that having to go without your usual luxuries is making some of you distrustful and unusually angry. That's something the other judges and I will have to look at when we review the tapes to decide who must leave this week."

Olivia's mouth dropped open. Then she snapped it shut.

"All right, this is the secret about Ripley." Veronica's tongue flicked across her lower lip. "It's something Ripley herself doesn't even know, since she has been deprived of TV and the Internet along with the rest of you." Veronica did another one of her pauses, then she turned toward Ripley. "I'm sorry to tell you this, but your mother entered a rehab clinic in Malibu yesterday morning."

"Ooooh," James called out. Like we were in school and someone had just gotten called to the principal's office. Dillweed.

Ripley's face paled, but she just gave a short nod.

"You should really see this as a positive thing," said Veronica. She reached out and touched Ripley's arm. "I just hope your mother won't try to leave too soon. You know what happened in this house." She gave a delicate shudder. "I'm sure it could have been prevented if Katrina Decter had only stayed in rehab long enough to make a complete recovery."

"What is she talking about?" Georgina asked Brynn.

Brynn didn't seem to hear her. It didn't matter.

Veronica was more than happy to answer. What had happened in this house ten years ago made good television.

"Katrina Decter was an actress on her way to superstardom when her husband killed her. Right in the great room upstairs," Veronica explained. "She was just out of rehab herself, and she had had a relapse. She actually attacked her little daughter, Nina, who was only four. Her husband killed her to save Nina's life."

"I don't think I have to worry about my mom trying to off me, if that's what you're saying," Ripley said sharply.

Veronica better back off, I thought. She was about to face off with Bad Ripley. And I had a feeling that if you put Veronica and Bad Rip into the cage together, Ripley might just walk out with Veronica's head in her hand.

"Aren't you sensitive," Veronica cooed. "That must be one of your deep fears coming out. It wasn't my implication at all."

Uh, yeah it was. It so was.

"Whatever," muttered Ripley.

"Let's move on. Georgina, now it's your turn to choose a contestant, and we'll hear one more secret," Veronica said. Her eyes flicked around the group. "I see some nervous faces," she commented. "It makes me wonder if I know what each of you is hiding."

Veronica strolled among us. "Who will it be, hmmm?" She tapped Brynn on the shoulder, and Brynn flinched. "Twitchy. I bet she's got something good."

She moved on and stopped next to me. I used my ATAC training to keep my body relaxed and a pleasant expression on my face. "And what about this all-American teen? He looks like his big secret is getting away with breaking curfew. But I know better."

I didn't allow myself to look at Frank. *She's just trying to build up the intrigue,* I told myself. *It's her job to make a good show. Make sure nobody gets busy with the remote during* Deprivation House.

"It's true. I'm really a girl," I joked. Lame, I know. But it was all I could come up with in the moment.

Veronica continued to walk from person to person. It was like some demented game of duck, duck, goose. "So, who will it be, Georgina?" she finally asked.

Georgina didn't hesitate. "Frank."

Accusations

She can't know, I told myself. *ATAC security is way too good. She can't have gotten past it.* I completely believed that. In my head. In my stomach, I wasn't quite as sure.

Veronica raised her eyebrows. "Interesting choice," she told Georgina. "And something of a bargain, because Frank's secret gives away something about Joe as well."

My palms began to sweat. A secret that was about me and Joe? How many things could that be?

Strategy. I needed strategy. What should Joe and I do if we were outed right here and now?

Deny it? Say it was some ratings stunt of Veronica's? Or something she and the other producers had come up with to create tension in the house? I don't watch a lot—or actually any—reality TV, but Joe says they all end up having lots of fights among the contestants. That was definitely turning out to be true on our show.

Or should we admit to the truth and warn everybody that they were in danger? Just explain that Joe and I had been placed undercover as contestants because the death threats they'd received were being taken very seriously—and for good reason, since two people in this house had already been victims of murder!

Veronica smiled at me. "Here's a secret about Frank and Joe," she said, breaking her long pause. "Joe's father makes twenty-eight times the salary Frank's does." She pretended to do the math on her fingers, her red nails flashing. "Let's just say there are quite a few dollars' difference."

Relief washed through me. I struggled to prevent it from showing on my face. Frank Dooley wouldn't be relieved to hear Veronica blabbing about how little money his family had in front of everybody. He'd be outraged. But he'd also probably be trying not to show that Veronica had gotten to him.

I jammed my hands in my pockets and locked eyes with Veronica. "It's not exactly a secret that his family is richer than mine." I jerked my chin toward Joe.

"True," Veronica answered. "But did either of you know there was that much of a difference? Every single year?"

I glanced over at Joe. He smirked at me and fingered the Diesel sunglasses he had stuck in his shirt pocket. He was enjoying himself a little too much. He'd better know he wasn't keeping those sunglasses after the mission was over. There would be no way to explain to Mom and Aunt Trudy how he'd gotten them.

"Dude!" James gave my brother a congratulatory smack on the back. "Guess it won't hurt you too bad when I win," he added.

"Joe drives a Corvette. Frank gets to borrow the family Toyota Corolla. When it's not in use. Or in need of repair," Veronica continued. "Last year Joe went on three vacations—Switzerland, the south of France, and Florida. Frank and his family went to visit his aunt Sharon in Boise, Idaho. For those of you who don't know it, and I imagine that's most of you, Boise's biggest attraction is, I believe, an extremely large potato."

"I think seeing a Super Spud sounds cool," said Olivia. I wasn't surprised that Olivia jumped in to take my side. Basically, Olivia thinks that if you're rich, you're a spoiled snob, and that if you're poor, you're a basically decent person. It was that black and white with her.

Veronica clapped her hands. "I'm off. The secrets should give you all something to talk about. Gossip is about the only type of entertainment you lambs have left, am I right?"

She didn't wait for an answer, just turned and strode back into the mansion.

"What a complete witch," Gail said, staring after her.

"Cameras," Hal reminded her.

"Right. They can't film twenty-four/seven because of the union rules about minors working on TV shows, but you know they had to have been filming when Veronica laid out all those secrets. And I'm sure they still are. They'd want our reactions."

Joe snorted. "I don't think you really have to worry about it, Gail. Veronica would probably consider being called a witch a compliment."

"At least you two didn't give her what she wanted," Gail told me and Joe. "You didn't start throwing punches."

"I don't have anything to be mad about," Joe commented, shrugging. "Am I supposed to be upset that my family has a lot more money than his?"

"He's your brother," Olivia snapped.

"We just met each other," Joe shot back. "I know him as well as I know you." He raked his hands through his hair. "It's not like I took something from him."

"The situation is what it is," I said. "I'm fine with the family I have."

"What about you, Ripley? Are you okay?" asked Brynn. "It must have been so hard hearing that about your mom, especially because we don't have our cells anymore. You can't even e-mail anyone to see if she's okay."

"You could drop out," James reminded her. "There are still cash rewards left for the next two people who do. You could scoop up the thirty thou dropout bonus, go see your mom. You've already done what you came here to do, right? Proved how nice you are."

"You just think you know why I'm here," Ripley said.

Huh. Interesting.

"And anyway, my mom will want her privacy," Ripley continued. "She won't want to see me until she's through the program."

"Sounds like you're familiar with the drill," Olivia observed. "I don't get how people with everything even get substance abuse problems. They have everything. If I had half of what your mom has, I'd be the happiest person on the planet."

Did she even hear herself? Her prejudice against rich people made Olivia as much of a witch as Veronica sometimes.

"Tell that to the little girl whose mother tried to kill her," Brynn muttered. "Both of her parents were pretty rich. Famous actor. Famous director. Living in this fancy house."

"You know what?" said Gail. "I'm starting to think this place really has been cursed since that director killed his wife here. Think about it: We had another accident during the competition today. Georgina's crash could have been a lot worse."

"The curse is something Veronica and the producers want us to believe in," Joe said. "They're trying to make the show more dramatic. Like that message we found in the Deprivation Chamber. A curse doesn't write 'Death House' on a wall. A person does that. Or am I wrong?"

"Did you forget the part about the demon?" asked Hal. "Nina's mother was supposed to have been possessed by a demon when she attacked Nina. That's why Nina's father had to kill her mother. A demonic spirit could write on a wall."

"I thought you were more into the science part of science fiction," I told him. Usually the only thing he talked about—or seemed to think about—was creating the specifications for L-62, the planet he was going to base a computer game on. He wanted to win the million-dollar *Deprivation House* prize to get the start-up money he needed for the game.

"There is scientific evidence that spirits exist. The energy they produce can be measured," Hal answered.

Brynn turned around and headed inside. "Where are you going, Brynn?" Ripley called after her.

"We've had this conversation a million times already," Brynn answered without stopping. I wanted to follow her. I pretty much wanted to be with Brynn every minute I could. I wouldn't be able to see her after the mission was over and I was back to being Frank Hardy.

But I couldn't leave now. I was afraid I'd miss something key. Our suspects were all gathered in one place.

"She was just out of rehab," Georgina reminded the group. "Duh. That's the only demon in the story. Her mom started using drugs again and went out of her head and attacked Nina. There's no demon and no curse."

"You don't know the number of bad things that have happened here," said Gail. "Two people died before you got here." She was referring to two of the production assistants. Leo had been killed by Mitch, and Sylvia had died of an aneurysm after Mary hit her over the head with a piece of wood.

"We know that Mitch and Mary were the ones behind everything that happened," Hal told her.

"'House of Death' was written in the Deprivation Chamber *after* Mary was taken away," Olivia pointed out.

"That's not the same as trying to kill people," I replied. "It's just a stupid prank." I wasn't at all sure that was true, but I wanted to chill everyone out.

"Disabling my brakes wasn't a stupid prank," Georgina said.

Silent Girl's eyes widened. Her name was Ann, but we called her Silent Girl because she hardly ever talked. It was part of her strategy. She didn't want to give away anything about herself, in case it could be used against her somehow.

"If I find out who it is, they are going to be in a world of pain," James threatened.

"You're the most likely candidate," Joe told him. "You're always bragging about how great you are and how you're going to trample the rest of us. But how many competitions have you won? And how loud did you whine when exercise equipment got taken away?"

"Yeah, you have to be running scared," said

George. "I can see you giving yourself a little *help*."

"You don't know anything!" James yelled. "You just got here. You're never going to last. The rest of us have had things taken away little by little. You and your sister have to deal with tons of things being gone from day one. No hot food. No Internet. No TV. No hot water. No books or magazines. You're never going to make it. Just drop out now. Take the consolation money and go."

"It would give you fewer people to sabotage," George shot back.

"If the reason you think I'm sabotaging people is because I want to win, then everybody should be a suspect," James growled. "You all want to win as bad as I do. You just aren't as honest about it." He strode into the mansion.

"Touchy," Olivia muttered.

"He's right, though," said Ripley. "If someone is still sabotaging us now that Mary's gone, it could be any of us. And I'm voting for you."

"Me? Why me?" Olivia protested.

"You've made it very clear you don't think any rich kids should be allowed to compete for the money," Ripley answered. "Why not try to knock Georgina out of the competition? She doesn't deserve to win—that's what you think, isn't it?"

Olivia blinked rapidly. She opened her mouth,

but she couldn't find words quickly enough.

"Don't bother. We all know it is. You've pretty much said so every day since you got here," Ripley continued. She turned to Gail. "And I know how much you need money. I almost wouldn't blame you if you were willing to cheat—I mean murder—to get it."

"I would never hurt anyone to win," Gail said, her voice low and hard. "Never."

Ripley shrugged. "I'm just saying, I can see it."

"Let's get out of here." Olivia grabbed Gail's arm, and they hurried inside.

"If I were you, I wouldn't be as okay as you act like you are. About my family having so much more money," Joe said to me. "I'd be overheated. I might be willing to, uh, bend the rules to get some cash." Nice work on our cover.

"I'm not you," I told him.

There was a long silence. Even though we were outside, it felt like all the air had been sucked out from where we were standing.

"So, great," George finally said. "What you're all telling me is that my sister and I are probably sharing a house with a killer."

Worried?

"I guess that is what we're saying," I told George. "We're probably living in a house with a killer. *Zoinks*, as Shaggy would say."

My joke got a few half laughs. More than it deserved. Because it wasn't that funny. And because the living-with-a-killer thing was truly scary.

Ripley let out a sigh. "So what should we all do for fun? That doesn't involve bleeding or poisoning or snakes or anything like that."

"Well, if you take away all that stuff . . . ," Hal said.

"That leaves us with practically nothing," said George.

"Charades?" Ann the Silent Girl offered.

That got real laughs from everybody. "Of course *you* want to play charades. You never speak. You'll probably kill at it. Uh, I mean, you'll probably beat us all," Ripley quickly corrected herself.

"I want to change these pants first," Georgina said. "I got a grass stain on them, and I have to try to get it out. They're my friend Carly's."

"All you girls better watch yourselves," George warned. "Georgina is always borrowing her friends' clothes, then wrecking them."

"No, I'm not. Don't listen to him. We share some DNA, that's all. He doesn't know anything about me," Georgina told us, rubbing at the grass stain on the knee of her purple jeans.

"Meet up in the great room?" I asked.

"Where else?" answered Hal.

As I led the way inside, I caught Frank checking the balcony that overlooked the fountain. Pretty much Brynn's favorite hangout.

I let the others go ahead of me, and dropped into step next to Frank, who was bringing up the rear. I couldn't talk to him for too long. It would look suspicious, especially after Veronica pretty much invited us to hate each other. But I figured we could grab a second. "Do you know where the Band-Aids are in the supply closet?"

"I guess I can show you," Frank muttered. "You're

probably so used to having people wait on you that you're helpless."

"You know you want to go after her," I said once we were inside the walk-in closet. It was one of the few places we knew for sure there were no cameras. There and the bathrooms.

"Who?" he asked.

"Did you just say *who*?" I shook my head.

"Okay, I know who," Frank admitted.

Here's the deal. I started crushing on Brynn from the first day we showed up at Deprivation House. And for once, a girl realized that I am truly the superior Hardy brother in looks, charm, and all other departments that matter. You got it: Brynn seemed pretty happy to hang with me. A lot.

The thing was, Frank was crushing on her too. Mad crushing. Like he should go out and write the girl a poem or something. And Frank's never that way. Usually he avoids girls, because he gets all blushy and stammery when he tries to talk to them. But for Brynn, he was willing to actually, you know, go up to her and try to speak. What could I do but step aside? I couldn't make Frank compete with my magnificence when his heart was practically breaking out of his chest whenever he saw Brynn.

"So go find her," I told him. "I can keep watch by myself for a while."

"Are you sure?" he asked.

"I know I'm the little brother, but I've had as much training as you—" I began.

"No," Frank interrupted. "Are you sure it's okay with you . . . about Brynn . . . that I . . ."

See, he even gets stammery when he talks *about* girls. "I'm sure, I'm sure," I promised. "Ripley actually seems to be getting into real nice mode instead of just camera nice mode. Maybe I'll let her experience the wonder of me."

Frank laughed. I've been trying to teach him when things are funny and when they aren't. He still hasn't quite gotten the hang of it.

"Here are the Band-Aids." Frank tossed me the box.

"Sorry, I couldn't find any antiblush cream for you, bro," I said.

He didn't laugh. See?

I walked out of the closet with a couple of Band-Aids clearly in my hand, in case the cameras were on and anybody cared. Then I headed up the S-shaped staircase and down the hall to the great room, this massive space that was like three or four living rooms combined. It used to have this awesome TV. Now, well, now it still had a great fireplace.

I plopped down on one of the sofas next to Hal. He and George were the only ones there so far. "Are we really going to have to play charades?" he asked. The same way he'd ask, "Are we really going to have to drink pickle juice?"

I shrugged. "Nothing else to do. But it's not like it's a challenge or anything. Veronica's not going to come in here and make you."

"Hey, let's psych the girls out," said George. "Let's say we want the teams to be guys against girls. We can write up the list of charade ideas right now and substitute them for whatever ones the girls team comes up with. Then we'll be able to guess the movie titles or whatever they are in seconds."

"Uh, but the girls will realize that we aren't guessing the stuff that they came up with. If you shout out a movie title that they didn't write down, they'll know we're cheating." Not that I was planning to cheat anyway. It was interesting that George was so up front about wanting to cheat, though—since we were all in a competition together.

"Oh, okay. Then maybe we could—" He stopped abruptly as Georgina and Ripley came in.

Georgina narrowed her eyes at her brother. "What were you just talking about?" she demanded. "He has his guilty face on," she told Ripley.

"Nothing," George said.

I wasn't getting into this one. I wasn't on a mission to make sure there was no foul play in charades.

"You were trying to figure out a way to cheat," she accused. "He is humiliatingly bad at charades. He never guesses anything," she added to the rest of us. "I'm sure he was afraid of shaming himself. He actually started crying once because he didn't know what one of the words he was supposed to act out even meant."

"I was *seven*!" George shouted. "Will you stop telling people these stupid stories?"

"When you stop doing stupid things," Georgina told him sweetly.

"I am going to be so happy to get away from you. As soon as I win the mil, I'm getting legally emancipated. I'm moving out. I'm never going to have to look at you again. Or Dad. That bloated control freak."

"Yeah, this is it. Dad's gone too far. Legal emancipation is the only option. I'm not even going home after I leave here."

"You'll have to," George told his sister. "Because you won't have any money to live on, so you'll be at home, seeing the face every day, hearing the lectures. I'll be in my own place."

"We'll see," Georgina told him. The words came out sounding like, *In your dreams.*

"No, you'll—" George started.

"Keep at it!" James called out as he entered the

room. "Go on and take each other out. It wasn't really fair that they brought you two in late anyway."

There was a serious edge of anger to his voice. Had James been so angry to have two new players in the game that he'd decided to try to take one out? He was almost lethally competitive.

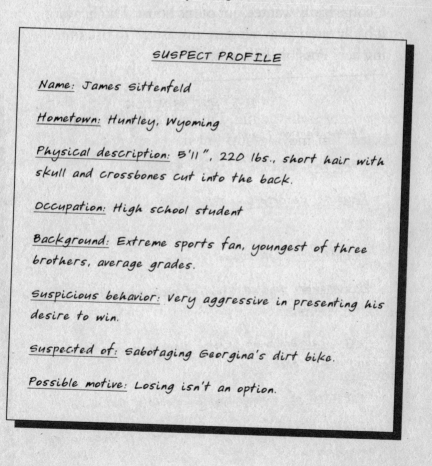

SUSPECT PROFILE

Name: James Sittenfeld

Hometown: Huntley, Wyoming

Physical description: 5'11", 220 lbs., short hair with skull and crossbones cut into the back.

Occupation: High school student

Background: Extreme sports fan, youngest of three brothers, average grades.

Suspicious behavior: Very aggressive in presenting his desire to win.

Suspected of: Sabotaging Georgina's dirt bike.

Possible motive: Losing isn't an option.

"Worried?" George asked. "You should be. Georgina would have kicked everybody's behind in the race today. She might not look like it, but she's a total extreme spots fan."

Interesting how George jumped to his sister's defense against an outsider. Also interesting how sure he'd been that she'd win today's competition. George badly wanted out of his house. Did he want it badly enough to sabotage his sister? To risk injuring her? Possibly killing her?

SUSPECT PROFILE

Name: George Taggart

Hometown: Charlotte, North Carolina

Physical description: 5'11", 170 lbs., blond hair, blue eyes.

Occupation: High school student

Background: Spoiled child of rich parents; Georgina's twin brother.

Suspicious behavior: Knows Georgina would have won dirt bike race.

Suspected of: Sabotaging Georgina's dirt bike.

Possible motive: Wants to win money to become legally emancipated.

FRANK

5

Deeply Disturbed

Strategy. I needed a strategy.

It's not that I can't think on my feet. I can improvise. I have to do it on missions all the time. But I'm definitely more comfortable with a well-thought-out plan. With maps and schematics and facts I can memorize before going into an unknown situation.

Talking to a girl I liked . . . that was pretty much uncharted territory. I'd had some crushes, yeah. But I usually avoided them, to avoid the embarrassment of turning into a guy who lost 60 percent of his capacity to think, and 80 percent of his capacity to form words.

And how I felt about Brynn . . . it wasn't a crush.

I think Joe got that before I did. I don't know how to describe it exactly—

JOE

Joe here to help my bro out. The way you describe it is *loooove*.

FRANK

Get out. This is my section. "Loooove" isn't the word I'd use. "Loooove" isn't a word at all. The word "love"—which *is* a word—isn't what I'd use either. But how I felt around Brynn . . . it was good. I should be able to say it better than that. All I can tell you is, the more I was around her, the more I wanted to be around her. And I wanted to be around her right now.

I didn't bother checking the basement. There was nothing down there. The bowling alley was locked. The exercise equipment had been removed from the gym. The sauna had been hacked up by a chain saw. I'd had to do the hacking. Don't ask. There's been way too much badness at this house in the past few weeks to go through it all.

I made a pass through the kitchen and the dining room, then decided to stop by the billiard room— the former billiard room—where the Deprivation Chamber was. The chamber was a booth with a camera in it where any of us contestants could go and vent about anything that was bugging us. I couldn't believe any of the real contestants here voluntarily went in there. You knew whatever you said was going to end up on TV.

But maybe Brynn had felt like venting. She'd seemed upset when she left the group.

I stepped into the room, my footsteps echoing on the polished wooden floor. The big room felt empty. "Brynn?" I called out, just to be sure. No answer. As I turned back toward the door, I caught sight of something white out of the corner of my eye. A sheet of sketch paper lying on the ground.

Probably one of Hal's drawings of L-62, I thought as I headed over to retrieve it.

The back of my neck prickled when I picked the piece of paper up. It wasn't one of Hal's drawings. It was some words written in what looked like a child's handwriting. It read HOUSE OF DEATH.

Exactly the same words that had been written on the chamber wall. The handwriting looked the same too. Was this a practice sheet?

I carefully folded the sheet of paper and put it in my pocket. I needed to discuss this with Joe. But first I'd find Brynn. I wanted to make sure she was all right. And, okay, I just wanted to be around her for a few minutes. I went upstairs and down the hall to the room Brynn shared with Georgina and Olivia. Gail and Olivia sat on Olivia's bed, their heads close together. "What are you doing in here?" Gail asked.

"The door was open," I said. "I was looking for Brynn."

"Haven't seen her," Gail told me. She shifted her body, shoving something behind her.

Which of course made me want to know what it was. I wouldn't be a detective if it didn't. I walked over and sat down on the bed across from them. "It was pretty intense down there with Veronica, wasn't it?"

"Veronica's not as bad as some other people," Olivia answered.

"Really? Veronica's pretty slimy," I said, not caring if this was getting filmed or not. I casually leaned back on the bed. I could almost see what Gail had hidden.

"Veronica didn't accuse us of murder today," Olivia reminded me. "That was the newly nicest person in the world. Ripley."

"My brother pretty much said the same thing to me after you left," I told her. "Everyone was accusing everyone. We're all freaked out." I rolled onto my side and propped my head on my hand.

Yes! I could see it now. Gail was hiding a sketchbook behind her. Could it be the sketchbook the sheet of paper with the note on it had come from?

"Hey, did you find Hal's sketchbook? He's been looking all over for it." A lie. But you've got to be a good liar when you're an ATAC agent. "You know how obsessed he is with his drawings of that planet."

"This one's mine," Gail said quickly. "Hal's not the only one who likes to draw. I take art for every elective I can. I even won a prize once for a poster I made. Got fifty dollars."

Gail wasn't such a good liar. She gave way too much detail. And she looked up as she talked, like she was trying to find the answers up in her brain.

"Cool," I answered. "Can I see some of your stuff?"

"No," Olivia answered.

I laughed. "Is she your manager?" I asked Gail.

"I already asked her if I could see," Olivia explained. "She told me she never shows anybody anything until it's completely finished, and she doesn't have anything done yet."

"Well, if you finish something, tell me," I said. I stood up. "I'm going to go see if I can find Brynn. Everybody's going to play charades in the great room, if you guys are up for it."

"I'm not ready to hang with Ripley right now," said Olivia.

"I think I'll stay here too," Gail told me.

I nodded and left the room. My brain was whirring as I mentally reshuffled Joe's and my suspect list. I decided I needed to bump Gail and Olivia up. There was something they didn't want me to see in that sketchbook. Was it where they practiced writing in that kidlike way? Were they teaming up to sabotage the rest of the contestants?

SUSPECT PROFILE

Name: Gail Digby

Hometown: St. Louis, Missouri

Physical description: 5'9", 145 lbs., sandy hair, brown eyes.

Occupation: High school student

Background: Oldest of three kids raised by single mother. Grew up in severe poverty.

Suspicious behavior: Trying to keep sketchbook hidden.

Suspected of: Sabotaging Georgina's dirt bike; writing the message in the Deprivation Chamber.

Possible motive: Winning the millions could change her
life and the lives of her family members.

SUSPECT PROFILE

Name: Olivia Gavener

Hometown: Homestead, Florida

Physical description: 5'7", 140 lbs., red hair, freckles,
brown eyes.

Occupation: High school student

Background: Oldest of five kids, family on welfare,
helps out with paycheck from fast-food job.

Suspicious behavior: Contemptuous of rich people;
always strategizing how to win.

Suspected of: Sabotaging Georgina's dirt bike; writing the message in the Deprivation Chamber.

Possible motive: Needs money to continue to help family and have a different life.

I took a fast look in the great room to see if Brynn had rejoined the group. Nope. I continued down the hall, deciding to try the library next. I'd run into Brynn there once. That's where I had my first real conversation with her. And actually, I had no plan or strategy then, because I didn't know it was going to happen.

Now that I thought about it, it had been easy to talk to her that day. Maybe that's what made what I felt for Brynn—whatever I should be calling it—different from a crush.

The library door was ajar, and I pushed it open. Brynn stood inside. For a second I felt like I was in free fall. Like I'd just done a bungee jump and the cord hadn't started to pull me back yet.

"This isn't a bad place to hang, even now that we've been deprived of all the books and magazines," I said from the doorway.

Brynn didn't answer. She didn't turn toward me. She was staring at one of the walls. I didn't remember there being a painting on it or anything.

I took a few steps toward her. Then I saw it. Someone had drawn in crayon on the pale wallpaper. Pressing down so hard in places that the paper had torn.

"What is that even supposed to be?" I asked, hurrying over to Brynn. One figure in the picture was clearly a little blond girl, drawn the way a little kid would do it. Big head. Stick neck. Those hands that look like mittens. The other . . . it was some kind of creature. Blank eyed, with claws almost as long as its body.

It took me a moment to realize that Brynn hadn't answered. I pulled my gaze away from the drawing to her. She was still staring at the wall, her eyes dull and blank.

"Brynn! Are you okay?" I touched her shoulder, and she started.

"Frank!" She blinked rapidly. "I didn't even hear you come in. I saw this"—she jerked her hand toward the drawing—"and it completely freaked me out."

"It is pretty creepy," I agreed.

"The way the demon is about to grab her." She shook her head hard.

"Demon? Is that what you think it's supposed to be?" I asked.

"I guess it could be a basic under-the-bed monster," she answered. "But with Veronica bringing up the story about Nina and how her father told her that her mother had been taken over by a demon . . . My mind just went there."

"Makes total sense. It's probably what whoever drew it wanted us to think," I said. "Somebody's trying to scare us. Keep us thinking about the curse, about the house's history."

"Well, it worked. I'm officially scared," Brynn admitted.

"Maybe it's something Veronica and the producers came up with. I can see them trying to add extra excitement," I suggested.

The motivation made sense to me. But there were a lot of puzzle pieces that didn't fit with that theory. The sketchbook Olivia and Gail really didn't want me to see, for one. Georgina's sabotaged brakes, for another. Trying to make us think the house was cursed was a lot different from actually putting a player's life in danger.

And there was still the glass that had been mixed with the ice in James's water. Mary had insisted she hadn't done that when the police came to take her away. She'd confessed to everything else. The e-mail threats. The dead bird. The wood rolling off the woodpile on top of me. Putting the rattler in Ripley's bed. Everything but the glass. Why bother to deny it, if she'd really done it? Still, the glass in the ice didn't seem like something Veronica and company would do.

"I don't see Veronica doing this," Brynn said.

"Really? Why?" I was curious to hear her take on the situation at Deprivation House.

Brynn reached down and flicked on a light switch at knee level on the wall. Weird place for it. The light made the drawing look even more unnatural.

She ran her fingers across it, then trembled as they snagged on a ripped piece of wallpaper. "This wasn't done by somebody rational, somebody thinking of TV ratings." She turned to face me. "Frank, whoever drew this is deeply disturbed. Truly, seriously unbalanced."

Silent Girl Screams

"I agree with Brynn," Olivia said. "Whoever drew that is one messed-up individual."

Frank and Brynn had called the rest of us down to the library. We were staring at the drawing Brynn had discovered.

"Either that, or one great strategy mastermind," Frank commented.

Was that aimed at Olivia? She was the player most concerned with strategy. She'd even organized a secret alliance. I only knew about it because Frank had told me.

Ann's deep into strategy too, I reminded myself. The whole reason she never talked was because she thought revealing any info about herself could give the competition an advantage.

"I'm sticking with my theory that the producers are behind all this demon curse stuff," I said.

"Yeah? I think one of you did it," James announced. "One of you standing in this room right now, acting all innocent."

"Does that include you?" I asked, interested to see what reaction I'd get. "You came back into the mansion pretty fast after Veronica played her I-know-a-secret game. What did you do? Maybe a little drawing." I jerked my chin toward the wall.

James had some . . . let's call them anger management issues, and the way the crayon had ripped into the wallpaper seemed Jamesian to me somehow.

"Have I entered a time warp? Didn't everyone just say all this stuff?" asked Hal. "Scary thing, accusations." He shook his head. "Clearly, talking about it isn't going to solve it. No one's going to confess. We're going to go around and around and around and get nowhere."

"You have something better to do, nerd boy?" James demanded. "I'm thinking you don't want to talk about it because you have something to hide." His eyes narrowed. "Who have we all seen drawing away the whole time we've been here?"

"Hal," said Olivia quickly.

"Those are schematics. Plans. They are highly

detailed and precise," Hal protested. "Nothing like what's on the wall. It looks like a kid drew it."

"Yeah," Frank agreed. "To me it seems likely that whoever wrote that message in the chamber drew the picture. That writing looked like it had been done by a little kid, and Hal's right about the drawing. It definitely seems like it was made by a child." He glanced over at Olivia and Gail, who were standing close together. "Or at least someone who wants to give that impression."

"So you're saying it could still be the nerd," James said. "Only he changed his style to get us off track."

"I didn't exactly—" Frank began.

"You know what?" Gail interrupted. "I just realized James wasn't the only one who left the group early after our little meeting with Veronica. Brynn, you left early too."

"You think Brynn made the drawing and then pretended to find it? That's extra twisted," Olivia said.

"Why are we thinking that the drawing had to have been made today?" I asked. "Did anyone go into the library before Brynn?"

"That's what we're trying to find out, boy genius," James answered. "Who came in and did the drawing."

"I mean did anyone—not the perp—come into the library earlier today?" I clarified.

"Perp. Now he's all hard-core." James sneered.

Shoot, I had to be careful not to be so obvious about my training.

"I didn't come to the library before now," Georgina answered.

I got no's and head shakes from everybody else. "So we don't know when the drawing was done. It could have been last night. That would make sense, since we're pretty sure the show doesn't waste the camera time it has filming us sleeping."

"So we don't know anything," said Gail.

"I still say it's someone in this room," James insisted.

"And I say he who smelt it dealt it," George answered.

James jerked his head toward George. "What is that supposed to mean?"

George raised his eyebrows. "I guess they don't teach analogies in public school. What it means is, you're the one who started all the accusations about the drawing. That's the 'smelt it' part. Am I talking slowly enough? And I think you're the one who actually did the drawing. That would be the 'dealt it' part."

"Want to see what I learned in public school?"

James asked. He didn't wait for an answer. He launched himself at George and knocked him to the ground.

"Smash his smug rich-boy face in!" Olivia shouted.

I knew she had an attitude about rich people, but—wow.

James pinned George with a knee to the stomach. "I learned how to fight!" James yelled. Then he slammed George in the jaw.

George pretty much just . . . squirmed.

I figured as a rich boy myself—at least as long as I was undercover—I had to step in. I rushed over and locked one arm around James's thick neck. A couple of moves and he was on his back, with my knee on his chest.

"Rich boys also take martial arts," I told him.

"That's right!" said George as his twin helped him off the ground.

Idiot. I shot him a look that I hoped he read as *I'm not going to save your pampered rear twice.*

"So, we're in agreement. We don't know who did this?" I asked the whole group the question, but I kept my eyes on James. He gave a tiny nod.

"I keep looking at the drawing," Olivia said. "Is it just me . . . or does the little girl kind of look like Brynn?"

"It's practically a stick figure," Hal protested.

"Same hair," Olivia pointed out. "And the way the nose is drawn, it looks like it turns up at the end, the way Brynn's does."

"And Georgina's," her twin observed. "She has the hair, too."

"I am now officially creeped out," Georgina announced.

I looked over at Brynn to see how she was reacting. She was staring at the drawing, her eyes almost glazed. Then she gave her head a hard shake. "I think I've looked at it long enough. I'm going to go take a special Deprivation House cold shower. I'm never taking hot water for granted again!"

After she left, Hal stepped closer to the drawing and ran his finger over the picture of the girl. "I don't see it."

"If the girl is supposed to be Brynn or Georgina, are we supposed to think that demon beastie thing is real too?" asked Gail.

"I hope so," James said. "Charades is way too boring. And we don't have any TV. If there's a demon in the house, I hope it makes an appearance. Can't they do your bidding if you sell them your soul?" He tilted his head back and threw out his arms. "My soul is up for grabs if you could arrange for a—"

"Stop it!" Ann shrieked.

We all stared at her. Ann hardly ever talked. Hearing her let out a scream like that was shocking.

"What's your impairment?" James asked.

"You can't invite a demon to come to you like that!" Ann cried. "It's not some joke. Don't you know how dangerous it is? The demon will take over your body, your mind. It will make you do horrible things. And when it finally leaves, you'll be insane. If your body doesn't completely give out. Do you want to die?"

Those were more words than Ann—formerly known as Silent Girl—had spoken the entire time we'd been at Deprivation House.

"That's messed up," Olivia said softly.

I was hit by what Olivia had said when she first looked at the drawing. *Whoever drew that is one messed-up individual.*

I didn't know if I'd call Ann messed up. But she'd definitely shown that she had some deep feelings the rest of us hadn't known about. Disturbing feelings. She'd hidden them really well. What else had she been able to hide?

SUSPECT PROFILE

Name: Ann Sommerfeld

Hometown: Plano, Texas

Physical description: 5'5", 120 lbs., brown hair, brown eyes.

Ann rubbed her face with both hands. "Sorry. I didn't mean to go off that way. It's just that what James was doing was so perilous. It really scared me."

"Maybe you should sit down," suggested Frank. "Do you want some water?"

"No, I'm fine," Ann answered.

"Maybe we should go back to the great room," I said. "We've seen what there is to see here."

"Yeah." Frank started for the door—and froze as a long, terrified scream blasted down the hall.

"It's the demon!" Ann cried. "It answered the summoning!"

FRANK

7

Ripped Apart

Brynn! I knew that scream had come from Brynn. I tore out of the library and down to the girls bathroom.

She stood outside with her back pressed tight against the door. Like she was trying to keep something trapped inside. "Are you okay? What happened?" I exclaimed.

"What's in there?" Georgina asked. The rest of the group had reached Brynn only seconds after I did.

Brynn opened her mouth to answer, then shook her head and simply stepped away from the door. "It's safe to go in?" I asked.

She nodded.

I slowly opened the bathroom door. I sucked in

my breath with a hiss when I saw what was inside.

"What's in there?" Georgina asked again, her voice louder and higher, more scared.

James, Joe, and Olivia followed me into the bathroom. "It's a bloody teddy bear," Olivia called. "It's so gross, you guys."

The bear had been clawed open. Its stuffing lay all over the floor. One of its eyes was gone.

Ann pushed her way inside. "The demon did this. They start small sometimes, before they have full power in this world. But that's what it wants to do. To all of us."

"The red stuff is just ketchup," said Joe. "You think the demon wants to cover us with ketchup?"

Ann didn't smile.

"Whose bear is it, anyway?" I asked.

"It's Brynn's," Ann answered.

Olivia's eyes widened. "Maybe I was right about the girl in the drawing looking like Brynn. Maybe the demon really is coming after her, like in the picture."

"Do you really believe in demons?" Joe asked.

"How can you doubt their existence after seeing this?" Ann swept her arm toward the teddy bear carnage.

"Humans are capable of doing something like that too," Joe commented.

"Don't tempt a demon to show its power," Ann warned, then left the room.

Joe raised his eyebrows at me. Then he gave a half smile. "Maybe somebody should go check on Brynn."

"Practically everybody's out there with her," said Olivia.

"I'll go see how she's doing," I said, trying to sound like it was no big deal.

"You do that," Joe said, his smile widening.

You know, while he can be annoying a large percentage of the time, Joe is actually a good brother.

Brynn hadn't gotten far. She was sitting next to the bathroom door, leaning against the wall. Everyone else stood around in clusters, talking quietly. It didn't look like another fight was going to break out tonight.

"Hey," I said to her. "You want to maybe go out on the balcony, get some air?" I knew the balcony was one of her favorite places.

"Air would be good. I think I forgot to keep breathing about half an hour ago," Brynn answered.

I reached down and grabbed her hand so I could help pull her to her feet. I got this little *jolt*. Kind of like a static electricity shock. Except in a good way.

"Crazy night, huh?" I asked as we started through the house.

"I really need to talk about something not here," Brynn answered. "Tell me some random thing about you. Anything."

I hesitated. I wanted to answer as Frank Hardy, not Frank Dooley. I wanted to be my real self with Brynn. But there'd always be this huge chunk of stuff I'd have to keep hidden. I couldn't talk about my actual family or town or school.

"Come on. Anything. I'm not asking for deep, dark secrets. This isn't a Veronica torture session," Brynn said. She opened the glass doors to the balcony, and we stepped out. "You can tell me your favorite flavor of ice cream if you want. I don't care. As long as you say something completely unrelated to Deprivation House."

I didn't see any reason why Frank Hardy and Frank Dooley couldn't have the same favorite ice cream, at least. We did share a tongue and taste buds and a stomach. "Vanilla," I told her.

"That's it? Just vanilla?" she asked. "Not Vanilla CocoMocho or Vanilla Nutso?"

"Just vanilla," I said. Joe's the one who likes his ice cream stuffed with candy and nuts and pretzel bits and all that. I'm always telling him there's no ice cream in his ice cream.

"I like my ice cream straight up too. Otherwise you can't really taste it." She braced her hands on the balcony railing and stared down at the fountain. "I do enjoy the cone, though. I never eat ice cream from a dish if I can help it."

"Yeah." I realized I wasn't having any talking-to-girls anxiety. Maybe because conversations with Brynn were a little . . . odd. Or maybe because she made me feel like I'd already known her forever.

"So are you going to reveal your favorite flavor?" I asked.

"Don't have one," Brynn answered. "Or maybe I do, but I don't like to admit it." She lowered her voice to a whisper. "I think it hurts the other ones' feelings." She laughed. "You're going to think I'm as wackadoo as Ann. I heard all that demon stuff she was saying when she looked at the bear." Her face turned serious.

"I thought we were having a no-Deprivation-House conversation," I said.

"It creeps in," Brynn answered. She sighed. "I end up thinking about the house and everything all the time. Like the demon story. I can't believe a dad would tell his little girl her mother was possessed by a demon."

I looked down at the fountain for a moment. They hadn't turned it off as a deprivation yet. It was lit up at night, and right now the water was glistening under the beams.

"Maybe he thought it was a way for her to understand her mother's drinking and drug use," I finally said. "Not that I think it was a good way. But maybe he was trying to get across the idea that when her mother was on those drugs, she wasn't the same person."

"You think the demon story started before the night of the murder?" Brynn asked.

I shrugged. "I'm just trying to make sense of it."

"So the mom—the actress—had just come back from rehab, but she immediately had a relapse and went after the kid. And the father had to kill her," Brynn said. "It's really hideous. Then the girl had to testify and everything. It's sick the way Veronica talks about it and makes sure it's all on camera."

I nodded. "If she and the producers are behind that drawing and what happened with your bear, it's even worse."

"Taking some family's tragedy and twisting it into entertainment. It's disgusting." Brynn threw her arms out wide. "I hope this is all getting on camera. I hope it makes the cut!" she added loudly.

"Did you know humans have forty-six chromosomes, peas have fourteen, and crawdads have two hundred?" It was the first thing that came into my head.

"That's so cool! Crawdads must be hiding some

truly superhuman powers," Brynn exclaimed. "Thanks for the subject change, Frank. Let's see if we can last five whole minutes without even thinking of all the creepy stuff in this place."

I was definitely up for trying. But I wasn't sure it was possible.

"Good morning, everyone," Veronica said as we sat around the table eating our cold cereal. We'd lost the right to hot food days ago. "Eat well. It's a competition day!"

"It's cereal," James grumbled. "How well can we eat?"

I was sure that comment would end up in the footage we'd be viewing before Veronica told us who was the next person to be eliminated. Staying at Deprivation House was all about being able to deal with the deprivations without getting whiny.

"George, that bruise on your face looks so painful," Veronica commented. "How did you get it?" I couldn't decide if Veronica's question was sincere. She knew a lot about what went on in the house. But even she couldn't see everything.

"Walked into a door," George muttered. Probably too embarrassed to admit he got hit.

"Oh. I'm relieved to hear it," Veronica said. "It looks more like an injury from a fistfight. And I'd hate to think there was any kind of friction between our contestants."

Now *that*, I knew, wasn't sincere. Veronica would love any kind of friction.

"Especially with today's competition," Veronica continued. "Your relationships with one another are going to be important." She smiled. "But I don't want to say too much. You'll have to wait until this afternoon. Meet me at the fountain at three." And she was gone.

As soon as Olivia had downed her cereal, she signaled for me to meet her in the supply closet. She got Hal and Gail to meet us in there too. "Okay," she said. "I think today's competition is going to involve teams. That's what I got from Veronica. What about the rest of you?"

"Possibly," Hal said. "But not definitely."

"I'm not saying it's definite," Olivia snapped. "I'm saying it's possible. Will you all agree with that?"

We all quickly agreed. Olivia was in complete drill sergeant mode.

"What the 'alliance' needs to do—oh, clearly Gail is part of the alliance now," Olivia began.

I wasn't sure "alliance" was exactly the right word. Maybe dictatorship?

"What we need to do is make sure the rich kids don't win the competition. An alliance member needs to win. If that means your individual team losing, fine."

"So you're saying we should sabotage our teammate if they aren't in the alliance?" Hal asked.

"Exactly," Olivia answered.

Was Olivia behind Georgina's accident? Was she behind the drawing and the message in the chamber? Was she trying to recruit some help right now? I wasn't sure. But I was definitely sure this was a bad idea.

"What's the point?" I said. Olivia narrowed her eyes at me.

"The point is what it's always been since we formed the alliance. To win. The whole enchilada. One of us right here is going to win the million, and we're going to split it four ways," Olivia explained impatiently.

The stress of the competition was getting to her. She hadn't been this irritable and bossy when she first asked me to join the alliance. Or maybe she has been, but she was just hiding it because she knew she needed to be nice until I said yes.

"I know the purpose of the alliance," I said, trying to keep annoyance out of my own voice. "But it doesn't really matter who wins the competition. It's just for the show. It doesn't actually have anything to do with winning or losing the money, if you think about it."

"Winning the competition means controlling the next deprivation," Olivia told me, speaking slowly, exaggerating each word, like she was trying to teach me to talk. "Controlling the deprivation gives us power. We can choose a deprivation that will really hurt the other side. I've been studying them. I know their weak spots. I know how to make them hurt."

O-kay.

Hal cleared his throat. "Uh, joining the alliance made logical sense to me." He did another throat clearing. He sounded nervous. "It greatly improved my odds of winning a significant amount of money."

I could hear the "but" coming. It seemed like Olivia could too. The muscles in her jaw had clenched.

"But," Hal went on, "I didn't know that being in the alliance would involve cheating. I'm not . . . comfortable performing any kind of sabotage."

"What you're saying is that getting your computer game up and running isn't that important to you," Gail told him. Olivia shot her a proud smile.

"I didn't hear him say that," I jumped in. "Have you thought about the fact that if we get caught cheating, we get booted? That means no money."

I figured that argument might mean more to Olivia and Gail than talking about right and wrong.

"Even if we didn't get caught, I'm not willing to

hurt somebody to win," Hal said, voice cracking.

"I didn't say hurt. I said make sure they don't win the competition," Olivia protested.

"And you think that can be done in a completely peaceful, nonviolent way?" I shot back.

"Are you saying you want out?" Olivia demanded.

"No. I'm just trying to get things clear," I told her. I definitely needed to stay in the alliance. The person Joe and I were looking for could be right here in this little group.

"What about him?" Gail jerked her chin toward Hal.

"I think I do want out," Hal said.

Good for him.

"Fine. Of course, we'll have to tell the others you were part of an alliance against them," said Olivia.

"What? Why? That will mess you up as much as me," Hal protested.

"It will mess us up. But not as much," Olivia answered. "Because we'll still have each other. We'll still have the alliance."

Hal stared at the ground. Olivia, Gail, and I stared at him.

"Well?" Olivia finally said.

"I'm in," Hal told her, without looking up.

"You did the right thing." Gail patted his shoulder, and Hal flinched. "Those other kids have tons of money. They've had everything their whole lives. It would be so unfair if one of them got a million dollars."

"Yeah. Gail's family doesn't always even have money for food and heat. I have to contribute the money I make frying burgers to keep our household going," Olivia reminded him. "It would be so wrong for somebody like Brynn to win over Gail. One of Brynn's shoes would probably pay Gail's family's rent for a month. I can't believe she lets Georgina borrow them." Olivia shook her head. "Not the point. The point is that rich people don't need to win. Between Frank and Joe, it would be completely unfair for Joe to get that money."

"Completely," Gail agreed. "We all heard what Veronica said. Joe's dad makes a million times more than Frank's. Frank probably would use the money for stuff like college." She looked over at me, and I nodded. "What would Joe use it for? A second car? 'Cause you know he already has one."

"You know it," Olivia said. "You must be so furious at him, Frank. Now that you know how he's been living all these years. I mean, don't you look at him sometimes and think, 'I would really like to kill my brother'?"

Psycho Teammate

"What did you tell her?" I repeated. "I just want to know."

"That's not the point," Frank answered. He shifted uncomfortably on his seat at the edge of the tub. I'd scored the closed toilet seat. It was the most comfortable spot in our "conference room."

"I'm giving you a heads-up," he continued. "If you're paired up with Gail, Olivia, and maybe even Hal, you have to watch out for sabotage. I don't know if Hal's actually going to do anything. But Olivia and Gail were pushing hard, and Olivia is definitely going to be watching him."

"I just want to hear what you told her when she asked you if you wanted to kill me," I said. Sometimes I can't resist torturing Frank a little.

He sighed. "You realize I'm undercover."

I waved my hand in a hurry-it-up motion.

"I told her that when I couldn't fall asleep I did sometimes imagine different ways that I could off you and get away with it," he admitted.

I laughed. "I've been doing that for years about you! Many of my scenarios involve cleaning supplies, because everyone knows you're way into cleanliness and I'm a slob."

Frank decided to take the mature route. Otherwise known as the boring route. "Just be careful, okay?" he said.

I nodded. "You have no idea what form this sabotage might take?"

"None. It's up to the individual alliance member. We act alone. If we get caught, we get thrown out of the contest alone," Frank told me.

"You think Gail or Olivia wrecked Georgina's brakes?" I asked.

"Definite possibility," Frank answered. "I think they should be high on our suspect list for anything bad that's directed at one of you rich brats."

It's so cute when Frank tries to be funny.

"I'm even thinking that Georgina and Gail could be behind that drawing in the library and the message on the chamber wall," Frank went on. "When

I went looking for Brynn yesterday, I found a sheet of paper from a sketchbook. Same words as on the Deprivation Chamber wall. Same handwriting. I figured it was a practice draft."

"Sketchbook, huh?" I said. "That makes me think of Hal right off. He almost always has his with him."

"That was my first reaction too. But then I went upstairs to Brynn's room, and I saw Olivia and Gail talking. Gail hid something behind her back. I finally got a look at it—"

"And it was a sketchbook," I finished for Frank. "It's interesting that Olivia's the one who pointed out that the girl in the picture looked like Brynn. That fits with the whole destroy-the-rich campaign."

"And it was Brynn's teddy bear that became a demon sacrifice. Freaking out Brynn would definitely throw her off her game," Frank added. "Olivia didn't say anything about the drawing or the bear at the alliance meeting. You'd think she'd want to make sure that Hal and I didn't get spooked along with Brynn and the rest of you. She should want us focused."

"Maybe there's an alliance within the alliance," I suggested. "Maybe the girls are playing the two of you guys. Maybe they're planning to use you to help eliminate some of the competition, but cut you out later."

"If Olivia wins, I think she's going to forget how to even pronounce the word 'alliance,'" Frank predicted.

"Joe, your partner for this competition will be . . ." Veronica smiled.

I got this ate-way-too-many-hot-dogs-way-too-fast feeling in my gut.

"Olivia," she concluded.

Of course. Perfect. The girl who wanted every rich person dead, dead, dead. Who thought my own brother probably fantasized about killing me.

This is a good thing, I told myself. *You're a highly trained ATAC agent. You can handle whatever sabotage Olivia decides to throw at you. You wouldn't want her paired with someone who didn't have any advance warning—or any skillz.*

Frank hates that word, just FYI. Skillz. He hates any word that has a *z* where he thinks there should be an *s*. I know way too many facts like this about my brother.

Veronica kept on matching up the pairs as we stood around her on the front patio. Here's how it laid down. Frank and Ann. She showed up for the competition looking like a goth girl ready for a night out. She'd made some kind of weird charm out of twigs and string and hair. But after seeing

Ann lose it last night, I knew she wasn't making a fashion statement. That stuff had to be antidemon protection. She was one scared weird girl.

Brynn and Ripley got teamed up. Georgina and Hal. I wondered if Hal would try anything to sabotage Georgina. It sounded like Olivia—with backup from Gail—had put some real fear into him.

"That leaves James, George, and Gail," Veronica said. "Hmmm. An odd number."

James's hand shot up. "I'll go solo," he volunteered.

"Why am I not surprised to hear that?" Veronica asked. "Why do I suspect that the words 'does not play well with others' were featured on many of your elementary school progress reports?"

I noticed George's hand go up to the bruise on his jaw. I'm sure he was praying that Veronica would go ahead and let James play by himself.

George didn't know Veronica that well yet, or he wouldn't have bothered. She liked to do things in whatever way would make the most people unhappy. "No, I think I'll give Gail the chance to prove what she can do on her own. Gail, you seem like something of a follower to me. This will be a good opportunity for you, I promise."

"It's not fair," Olivia muttered.

"There's nothing in the rules requiring fairness

on the producers' side," Veronica stated, looking pleased with herself. She turned to James. "That means you and George will be a team."

"Good," George said quickly.

He'd figured out that attitude was the difference between staying at Deprivation House and getting kicked out.

James rolled his eyes but managed not to say anything that the judges wouldn't like when they were deciding who had to hear the words, "You are deprived of the chance to win one million dollars," during the next elimination.

Still, I was pretty sure that if team James-George lost today, there'd be another fight to break up. Cameras on or not.

"Now, on to the competition," Veronica said. "Perhaps those of you with families wealthy enough to hire help have heard that some house cleaners don't do windows. Perhaps even those of you whose families don't have so much in the bank haven't had to wash windows either. Maybe your parents take on that chore."

"Or they leave them dirty," George said under his breath. "Poor people don't mind being dirty, do they? Or is it that they can't afford soap?"

I felt like punching the guy myself. Just because I was undercover as a rich kid didn't mean I couldn't think he was a complete wad. Did it?

I reminded myself that I wasn't here to teach George Taggart manners. Or James. Or anybody else. I was here to stop a murder. The lives of every contestant had been threatened.

"As you may have noticed, we have lots of windows at Deprivation House," Veronica continued. She flicked one hand in the direction of the mansion. Oh, man. I can't believe I hadn't noticed before. It looked like somebody had sprayed down each of those windows with an oily, gray-green goop. I didn't especially want to think about what it was.

"We have so many windows that I guarantee each of the teams will get a chance to wash some," Veronica told us. "At least those teams that want a chance at winning today." She clapped her hands. "What are you waiting for? Go ahead and get started!"

"With what?" Georgina asked.

"Look around," said Veronica. "There may be some useful items lying about."

"Forget that," said James. "I'm getting to work right now." He raced toward the house, pulling off his T-shirt off as he ran. He used the shirt to scrub the glass of the closest window. All that happened was that he smeared the goo around—and got his shirt covered with the gunk.

"Idiot!" George shouted at him. "You're already losing us time. Help me look for something that will actually work!"

The rest of us were already looking. I spotted a bucket hanging from a branch of one of the trees. A branch very near the top. Of course.

"I'll go get that," I said to Olivia in a low voice. I gave my chin a quick jerk toward the bucket. I didn't want to give away its location to anyone else.

"I'll help," Olivia volunteered.

"That's okay. I got it," I said quickly. I definitely didn't want any "help" from Olivia when I was that far off the ground!

I didn't wait for her to answer. I took off in the direction of the tree—not going straight for it.

"Remember that the windows of the upper stories do count!" Veronica called.

I guessed I also needed to look for a hidden ladder. And some sponges. That should get us started.

I made a sharp turn toward the tree. A second later I was climbing. I could see the branches shaking below me. Somebody else had spotted the bucket. I glanced down. Olivia!

"I think I can get this one solo," I called down to her. "See if you can find some cloths or sponges or something. Or something we can use for a ladder."

"I think I see a sponge by the bucket," Olivia answered.

I squinted up at the top of the tree. Didn't see anything spongy. "I'll get it while I'm up there," I promised.

"Do you see where I mean?" Olivia asked. She kept climbing. So did I.

"Uh, I think so." Lie. Which made us equal. I was pretty sure Olivia was lying about seeing any sponges up there. Either she was trying to slow us down, or she was trying to get a chance to shove me out of this tree.

"Just go! I'll find it when I'm up there, I'm sure." I was pretty far up there already.

"Hal, get that mini tramp!" Georgina shouted from below. "George is a trampoline fiend! He'll destroy us on that thing, bouncing up to wash the second-floor windows."

I took a glance down. Bad strategy. It was a good idea to nab something the opposition could use to a big advantage. But Georgina had basically announced the location of the tramp to her brother—and he was a lot closer to it than either Hal or Georgina was.

"George! I saw it first!" Georgina shrieked. Like that mattered.

I got my attention back on my own prize and kept

climbing. There weren't too many great branches in this part of the tree. I picked one I *thought* would hold me, and jammed my foot on it. . . .

At the same moment Olivia decided to reach up and use it as a handhold. She jerked the branch back, and my foot was suddenly slamming down into empty space. A second later, my entire body weight was hanging by one hand.

"Look out!" Olivia yelled.

Look out. Yeah. For psycho teammates.

I managed to wrap my other hand around the branch, then haul myself up until I could straddle it. Don't doubt that I was hugging the trunk with both arms at that point. The branch I was perched on wasn't much stronger-looking than the one Olivia had managed to bend back.

"Hey, I see a pair of stilts. Over in the empty pool. We can use them to reach at least some of the higher windows. I've totally got the bucket and whatever else is up there," I told Olivia. "Or you can keep climbing and I'll go for the stilts."

It would look totally suspicious if she thought we should stick together now. Another team could get the stilts—and a big advantage. I knew she wanted our team to lose. But she didn't know I knew, and she didn't want me to know. Got it?

"I'll go," Olivia said. And she started climbing

down. A lot more slowly than she'd gone up. I liked the new sabotage method. Slowness. No pain involved for Mr. Joe.

I scrambled up the next couple of branches. They trembled under my feet, but without any assistance from Olivia, they stayed steady enough to stand on. I grabbed the pail and did a sponge check. None. Knew she was lying.

As I started down the tree, I did a check of the area below me. Olivia hadn't made it to the stilts, but George was already bouncing on the trampoline, trying to get high enough to reach the second-floor windows. James was using a big palm frond to scrape gook off one of the bottom windows on the first floor. For two guys who hated each other, they were a decent team.

George came down on the tramp, and I noticed it sagging. Sagging way more than it should have with just one person on it. "George!" I shouted as loudly as I could. "Get off the trampoline. There's something wrong."

He didn't hear me.

I moved from branch to branch faster. I took time for another fast look at George. Couldn't he feel that something was wrong with the trampoline? I leaped the last five feet down and hit the ground at a run.

"George!" I yelled. "Get off of that!"

"We've got him worried!" James called up to George.

George grinned, did a one and three-quarter somersault, landed on his back, then let the bounce take him to his feet. The bottom of the trampoline had almost touched the ground on the last bounce.

"Show-off!" Georgina yelled.

George grinned wider and started to do the move again. A somersault. A three-quarter. But when he landed on his back, he didn't bounce. The trampoline didn't hold his weight, and he fell straight to the ground.

And lay still.

Another One Down

A nn grabbed her charm in both hands. So hard I could hear some of the twigs it was made of snapping. "It's the demon curse!" she cried.

"Come on, Ann. It was an accident," I told her. Honestly, I wasn't sure about the accident part. But I was sure a demon wasn't involved.

I rushed over to where James was lying. Ripley was crouched beside him, most of the rest of the group gathered in a loose circle around them. Georgina had her fingers pressed to her lips as she stared down at her brother. His face was pale, his eyes only half open.

"George, can you hear me?" Ripley asked.

"Yeah," George croaked out.

"Don't try to sit up," she ordered. "Can you move your fingers and toes?"

She'd clearly had some training. She was launching into the check for a spinal injury.

I watched George closely. He was able to move his toes and fingers as soon as Ripley asked him to. Good.

Then a not-so-good thought struck me. Ripley had been the first one to come to the rescue. The same way she had when Bobby T had his allergic reaction and when the dog attacked Joe. Was she just trying to make herself look like a hero on the show? If she got some good PR, her parents would keep supplying her with cash and clothes and, I don't know, whatever girls want.

Ripley didn't plan the allergic reaction or the dog attack, I reminded myself. Mitch had been behind both of those. But if Ripley felt like she needed even more good PR, would she create the situations that would let her get it?

I ran my eyes over the trampoline. The thing looked brand-new. Which made sense. *Deprivation House* should spring for new equipment, even though they were trying to make us live with as little as possible. It was a safety issue.

So why hadn't the trampoline held George's weight? A ten-foot tramp like that one should easily handle someone his weight. I had another not-so-good thought. A thought I'd been having too often lately: sabotage.

SUSPECT PROFILE

Name: Ripley Lansing

Hometown: Malibu, California

Physical description: 5'10", 140 lbs., straight brown hair, blue eyes.

Occupation: High school student/heiress

Background: Only daughter of rock star dad and cosmetics company CEO/owner mom. One older brother, one younger. The wild kid of the three.

Suspicious behavior: Often the first one to reach an injured person, winds up being the "hero."

Suspected of: Sabotaging contestants so she can save them.

Possible motive: Needs to improve her bad-girl public image or she'll be financially cut off until she's thirty.

But had Ripley had time for sabotage? Had she managed to find out ahead of time what the challenge was going to be—or at least that the trampoline was going to be involved—and loosen the springs or distress the canvas in some key places?

Or could she have found the trampoline first, done some fast damage, and left it for someone else to find and hurt themselves so she could come to the rescue?

"Ripley, out of the way, please. Let the medic take over," Veronica called as she strode toward us.

"I've got it," Ripley answered.

"Yes, I'm sure a high school girl who spends more time at movie premieres and concerts has the equivalent of a medical degree," Veronica shot back. "Move, please."

Ripley stood up and backed away.

"Is he going to be okay?" Georgina asked.

"It doesn't matter," Ann muttered. "It's the curse. Bad things are going to keep happening until we're all dead." She stroked the charm.

Is it impolite to say that I liked her a lot more when she wasn't talking? At least she wasn't one of the rich kids. I didn't have to try and make it look like I was sabotaging her to keep Olivia and Gail off my back. Even if I did something really mild, it could send Ann over the edge. She was so freaked already.

The medic carefully checked George out. "He looks good," she told Veronica. "Maybe a little aspirin. Some ice for any sore spots."

"So I can stand up?" George asked. He didn't wait for an answer. Just shoved himself to his feet with a grimace.

"That's all for today, everyone," Veronica announced. "This competition is canceled."

"Unfair," James told her. "George and I were clearly going to win."

There were all kinds of "untrue's" from pretty much everyone in response.

"The competition had just gotten started," Olivia protested. "Just because you were slightly ahead—"

"Slightly! Did you say *slightly*?" James interrupted.

"Why can't we—" Gail began.

"This is not up for debate," Veronica told us. "The competition is over. We will have a new competition tomorrow."

"Can't we just start right where we were tomorrow? With a new trampoline?" George asked. "I'll be fine."

"Everything is not all about you, George," said Veronica. "Although after reading your father's letter, I'm not surprised you think it is. The element of surprise was key to this competition. We can't regain that. There will be a new competition tomorrow. I have nothing more to say." She turned and walked inside the mansion.

As soon as she was gone, George faced off with James. "This wasn't enough for you?" he asked, touching the bruise on his jaw.

"What are you talking about?" James demanded.

"There is no way that trampoline wasn't messed with," said George. He started to crouch down to inspect it, but his sister got there first.

"Definitely messed with," Georgina announced. "The canvas is cut away from the springs. About every other one." She walked over to her brother and stood close to him. "You know what? I'm starting to think there are people here who aren't happy they got handed some new competition this late in the show. First I get a bike with death brakes. Then you get the killer trampoline."

Good theory. Except how could anyone know that George was going to end up on the trampoline? I didn't say anything. It seemed like one of those situations where listening was the best strategy.

"I'm satisfied with the spanking I gave you last night," James told George. "If you think I care more about handing down a little more punishment to some rich kid than winning a million dollars, you're insane. I would never betray a teammate. Never."

You know what? I believed him. James is competitive to the nth degree. I couldn't see him doing anything to hurt his chances of winning, no matter how much he hated somebody.

"He couldn't have known that George would end up with the trampoline, anyway," Hal put in. "And James couldn't have sabotaged it once George had brought it over to the mansion to start on the windows. George would have seen him."

"Thank you, Hal," said James.

"Not taking sides," Hal muttered, eyes on the ground. "Just being logical."

His logic matched mine.

"So somebody sabotaged the trampoline without caring who would end up being the victim," Olivia said. The girl was all about strategy. She was good at putting herself in the mind of the perp. Because she *was* the perp? And trying to work some fake-out on the rest of us by bringing it up?

"It's the demon!" Ann burst out.

"The cuts are pretty neat," Ripley observed. "They don't look like they were made with huge, hideous claws."

"You people have to stop mocking! Is somebody going to have to die before you stop?" Ann cried. She dashed into the house.

"Maybe freak girl snapped and did it herself," James said.

"She's not a freak," Brynn told him.

James raised one eyebrow. "What would you call her?"

Brynn hesitated, then shrugged. "What I'm saying is, everybody's afraid of something."

"You know what I'm afraid of?" Ripley asked. We all looked at her, waiting. "I'm afraid of what's going to happen at tomorrow's competition."

"Good afternoon, and welcome to the replacement competition," Veronica said to us the next day. She'd had us all gather in the dinning room.

"What's with the chef's hat?" James called.

Veronica adjusted the tall white hat she was wearing. It was an odd match with her pale blue suit and spike heels. Even I've absorbed enough about fashion to know *that*.

"If you had better manners, you'd already know," Veronica told him. "I was about to explain, before you interrupted, that today's competition involves cooking skills."

"Are we still having teams?" Olivia asked.

Veronica let out a small sigh. "Yes. Perhaps you and James should ask some of your other housemates to review what they learned in charm school.

I'm sure some of them were sent," she answered.

"Same teams as last time?" George wanted to know.

"Even if it seems that they learned nothing," Veronica added. "Yes, same teams. No more interruptions, please. Or I will simply cancel today's competition as well and choose the next deprivation myself."

The room went silent.

Veronica smiled. "Today you will be making pies. And, as a special treat, you will be able to eat the pie you make. I know many of you have missed your desserts."

Nobody spoke. I think everybody was still afraid Veronica would take over choosing the deprivation. She chose a lot of them anyway. We didn't only get stuff taken away after a competition. But with a competition, there was a chance you'd win and get to pick something to lose that you didn't care about too much.

"You'll find everything you need—or at least everything you may use—out on the back lawn," Veronica concluded. "Go!"

We went, racing through the house and out the back doors onto the sloping lawn. There were six tables with pie-making ingredients laid out on them.

"Is there strawberry? I would kill for a strawberry pie!" Ripley exclaimed. "Not really, you guys! You know what I mean."

I didn't care about flavor. I just wanted to get started. I dashed to the closest empty table. Apple. "This okay?" I asked Ann.

"I don't care." She'd added a second charm. Her face was pale, and there were dark smudges around her eyes.

"George, you know I love peach. Come on! Chose another table," I heard Georgina cry.

"Fine, fine. I'm not getting between you and your stomach," her brother answered. "Then I would end up dead."

"Why is everyone joking about it?" Ann's voice cracked as she asked the question.

"Because they're scared too," I told her. "It's a different way of dealing. You want to find the recipe for apple pie in there?" I nodded toward the cookbook. Then I realized there were no measuring cups, no mixing bowls, nothing to stir with, no baking pans.

"What are we—? Are we supposed to use our hands or what?" Olivia called out.

"Finally, an intelligent question." Veronica had followed us out to the lawn at a slower pace. "I'm sure you're all familiar with the green movement.

Around the corner, in the formal garden, you'll find a variety of materials that, if recycled creatively, should provide you everything you need."

"Can we use the ovens in the house?" asked Georgina. I hadn't even thought about ovens.

"No," Veronica answered. Just no. With one of her Veronica smiles.

"Guess we'll have to build a fire," I told Ann. "I can deal with that. I was a Boy Scout." And a current ATAC agent with wilderness survival training. "But first we should grab supplies before all the good stuff is gone." I followed the group running for the garden.

"It looks like they moved a whole garbage dump over here," Brynn commented, staring at the mound of . . . who even knew what. Whatever it was didn't stink, so at least it was clean garbage.

Olivia started climbing straight up the heap. "I'll find stuff. You stand guard over the pile we make," she called to Joe. "We can definitely use this!" She picked up a glass goldfish bowl and hurled it at Joe. If it had hit him in the head . . . But he caught it.

I realized I was just standing there, keeping an eye on little brother. He could take care of himself. And Frank Dooley wouldn't be worrying about Joe Carr. Frank Dooley would be worrying about winning.

So I began circling the pile. I didn't think climbing on it was the best strategy. I figured it would be best to spot useful stuff from the ground. I did an Ann check. She had an iron poker in one hand. Okay, might be good for stirring if we were desperate. Could help with the fire. She was all right. I hadn't been sure she was going to be able to keep it together, for the competition or anything else. But she seemed all right.

I gathered up a couple of Frisbees and some foil. Combining them might make pie pans. They'd be better as pizza pans, but hey. I grabbed a plastic doll head that looked like it would hold just about eight ounces. So there was our measuring cup. I took a wooden bird, a wooden bat, and a wooden chair. That would be more than enough for fuel.

"I'm making a trip back to the table," Ann said. "I've got as much as I can carry."

"Looks like you found a bowl-like object." She had a plastic football helmet under one arm. "Want to take my measuring cup and start mixing? I want to find a couple more things, then I think we're good."

"Sure," Ann answered. I tossed her the doll head, and she actually almost smiled. I turned my attention back to the garbage heap.

"I call that ceiling fan," shouted James.

"You can't call. There's no calling!" Ripley shouted back. She was closer to the fan and grabbed it.

"Okay, keep it. I call that wagon wheel." Ripley got there first too. She staggered under the wheel's weight as she hauled it out from under a Styrofoam reindeer.

James laughed as she started rolling it back toward the tables.

"You didn't want that, did you?" George asked.

"Nope," James answered. "Didn't want the fan, either."

"My partner," said George admiringly. They slapped a high five.

"See, I am a good guy to—"

He was interrupted by a shrill scream of agony.

Targeted

A girl screamed again. The sound sent a bolt of electricity through my body. I half scrambled, half slid down the pile of junk and raced toward the tables. That was the direction the scream had come from.

I rounded the corner of the mansion, Frank and a couple of the others right behind me. Immediately, I saw Georgina sitting on the ground with both hands pressed over her mouth. She rocked back and forth in pain.

"Milk!" Ripley yelled from her spot at Georgina's side. "Somebody go get her some milk! She's been poisoned. We need to dilute it."

"I'll get it." Brynn started for the house at a run.

"Wait," cried Gail. "Different kinds of poisons need different treatments. We could end up hurting her. Just wait. The medic is going to be here in a second."

"What happened?" I cried, skidding to a stop in front of them.

"The demon!" Ann shouted. She stood at her own table, not taking a step closer to the rest of us. "The demon did this."

"Georgina ate a piece of peach from her table and it burned her tongue," Ripley answered. "Show them."

Georgina lowered her hands. She let out a whine as she opened her mouth. Think of the worst burn you've ever gotten from eating pizza when you're too hungry to let it cool enough. One of those hot, oily cheese burns that takes off a layer of skin. Then triple that.

Even standing several feet away from her, I could see that Georgina's tongue looked like raw meat. Oozy and puffy.

"That definitely looks like a corrosive poison," I said. I wasn't sure Joe Carr would have that kind of knowledge. He was more the guy who could tell the price of a pair of sunglasses with one glance. But this was important. And Ripley, who was the most privileged of us privileged rich kids, obviously knew something about first aid. "That means we definitely don't want to make her throw up."

"Yeah, I accidentally drank some toilet bowl cleaner once," George said, staring down at his sister. "They said throwing up would wreck my throat."

"How do you accidentally drink toilet bowl cleaner?" asked James.

"I was five. I liked the color. I guess I drank it on purpose. But I didn't, you know, drink poison on purpose," George answered.

"Here's the milk!" Brynn called.

"Don't give it to her," I said. "I think there are some poisons where you shouldn't give the person anything." Actually, I was positive. "We don't know what she took. We've got to wait for the medic."

"I'm here," the medic called. "Back up and give me some room."

We all backed up a little, but stayed close. Except Ann, I mean. She still hadn't moved closer to the group.

"What did you take?" the medic asked Georgina.

"Noting," Georgina answered, her voice thick and distorted. "Ust peach." She flapped her hand toward the table where she and Hal were going to make their pie.

Hold up. Hal. Had Hal poisoned the peaches?

From what Frank told me, Gail and Olivia had leaned on Hal pretty hard. They'd pretty much told him that if he got a rich partner and didn't do what he had to do to make sure the rich kid lost, they'd hang him out to dry.

SUSPECT PROFILE

Name: Hal Sheen

Hometown: Coshocton, Ohio

Physical description: 5'8", 150 lbs., straight brown hair, brown eyes.

Occupation: High school student

Background: Mensa member, statewide science fair winner three years in a row.

Suspicious behavior: Was Georgina's partner when she was poisoned.

Suspected of: Sabotaging contestants who aren't part of the alliance.

Possible motive: Threatened by Olivia to do sabotage for good of the alliance.

"I want to get Georgina to a hospital ASAP," the medic told Veronica. "I don't think she ingested much of the substance. The abrasions don't continue deep into her throat."

"Pit it ou," Georgina said.

"She spit it out," George translated for his sister.

"Even so," said the medic. "I don't want to take any chances."

"I've already called an ambulance," Veronica announced.

An ambulance. Again. Bobby T had needed an ambulance before he'd been booted from the show.

At least he'd come back alive. We'd had a couple of people, both crew members, leave Deprivation House in silent ambulances. No sirens because there was no rush. The patients inside were already dead.

Today's ambulance ride wouldn't be one of those. But that didn't mean we'd had our last.

"What have we got?" Frank asked. We were back in our "office" late that night. I'd managed to call toilet seat again. Yes! The edge of the bathtub is hard. And cold.

"We've got a poisoning, the sabotage of a trampoline, sabotaged brakes, a drawing of a demon, and a partridge in a pear tree." I sang that last part. Frank didn't even smile.

"All that since Mary was removed from the house." Frank shook his head.

"And the perps keep on comin'," I said.

"Do we think this is the work of one person?" Frank asked.

"Usually I'd say it would be really unlikely that more than one person in our little community had turned homicidal," I answered. "But since we've already had to oust two wackos . . . Who's to say there's only one more?"

"Hal seems like a possibility," said Frank.

"I was thinking the same thing. Do you think he would have gone that far to keep Olivia and Gail happy?" I replied.

"They basically made it a choice between keeping them happy and losing the chance to split the million dollars with them," Frank mused. "Hal really wants start-up money for his game."

"Poison, though. He could have done something a lot less hard-core, right?" I asked. "I mean, Olivia threw a goldfish bowl at my head and tried to help me out of the top of a tree. He could have done something medium-core like that."

"I agree," Frank answered. "He's a possibility, but not top of the list, I don't think. Also, if he is behind the poisoning, then we definitely have two people at work. There would be no reason for Hal to seriously hurt George. That wasn't anything Olivia and Gail were expecting from him."

"No reason for him to have sabotaged Georgina the first time either. Olivia and Gail hadn't threatened him yet." A new thought hit me. "Or else Hal's a lot more sly than we're giving him credit for. Maybe he wanted to take some of the competition out all along. Maybe he was working on it before Olivia and Gail even brought it up. Maybe he damaged the dirt bike's brakes, and tried to poison Georgina, and messed up George's trampoline."

"Why not just admit he sabotaged the brakes when Olivia brought up sabotage?" asked Frank.

"Maybe he didn't want to give them any info to use against him. Maybe he's planning on playing the alliance somehow," I suggested. "Maybe he even did the demon drawing. He's always carrying around a sketch pad, and the practice handwriting you found was on sketch paper."

"But Gail and Olivia were trying so hard to keep their sketch pad hidden from me. Why do that, if there was nothing to hide?" Frank asked.

I shrugged. "Maybe they were trying to hide something else. Like . . . that they'd been drawing pictures of me! Yeah, they didn't want you to know that they think I'm the more handsome brother. They thought it would hurt so bad, since I'm already the rich one."

"Yeah, I'm sure that's it." Those were the words Frank said. But somehow they came out sounding like, *Only in your delusional skull, my brother.*

"I'm just saying that there's more than one reason to keep the sketch pad hidden. It doesn't mean they wrote the note or did the drawings," I clarified. "So, we got Hal. Who else?"

"James. The guy wants to win. We know that. He never lets anyone forget it," Frank answered.

"I think we'd need a two-perp scenario with James, too. Because I really don't believe he'd sabotage his teammate. Not that he cares about sportsmanship or anything like that. But, like you said, he wants to win," I said.

"Olivia and Gail are clearly good suspects. All the victims we've had since Mary left have been rich. Two attacks on Georgina, one on George. It was Brynn's teddy bear that got shredded, and maybe it was even supposed to be Brynn in the picture." Frank stood up. I could tell he wanted to do some pacing, but there wasn't space in the bathroom.

"I never even think of Brynn as being one of the rich kids," I said.

"I don't either. Olivia was saying stuff about her

shoes. I guess they're expensive. I wouldn't know," Frank admitted.

"Don't look at me," I protested. "I know my shades, yeah. And sneakers. But that's about it."

Frank sat back down. "So Olivia and Gail may be working together. Maybe either Olivia or Gail is working separately. Gotta say, Gail seems less likely. She seems to be a follower type."

"I'm with you. I think Olivia should be at the top of our list," I agreed. "And we should be thinking about Ripley, too. She's been right there next to two of the accidents. Giving instructions on how to take care of Georgina. Checking George for spinal injuries. She wasn't right on the spot when Georgina crashed, but that would have been hard to accomplish. You and Georgina were flying. Ripley was near the back of the pack."

"Georgina. George. Georgina," Frank said slowly.

"It seems like their dad has kind of the ego," I commented. "He basically named both his kids after himself."

"Georgina. George. Georgina," Frank said again.

"What about Ann? You were partnered with her. Has she snapped or what? Do you think she could—" I began.

"George thought maybe somebody was going

after him and his sister because they were the new people," Frank interrupted. "It is kind of strange that they've been targeted repeatedly."

I tapped my head. Sometimes it helps me shake thoughts loose. Didn't work so much this time. "None of the people we've talked about have a reason to focus on George or Georgina. Yeah, they're rich, and that makes Olivia and Gail insane. But there are other rich people around."

I did another couple of taps. A thought came loose. "And anyway, even though it seems like the G's were targeted, they couldn't have been."

"Why not?" Frank asked.

"Because no one knew it was going to be George who ended up on the trampoline or Georgina who would end up with the peaches and the bad brakes," I explained.

We both sat in silence for a moment.

"You remember how you said you'd know how to kill me because I'm your brother?" asked Frank.

"I don't think I said it exactly like that," I objected.

"Okay, but you said something like you'd make it look like an accident involving cleaning projects, because I like to clean and it wouldn't look suspicious," Frank went on.

"How did we go from talking about George and

Georgina to talking about me and you?" I asked.

"They're siblings, just like us," Frank answered.

"Not just like us. One of them is a girl," I said. "Oh, well, maybe just like us."

Frank rolled his eyes. "What I mean is, you know the people you're related to really well."

Another thought came loose, and I didn't even have to tap my head. "Like that your sister loves peaches. And the color purple. There was only one purple dirt bike, and she went right for it."

"Georgina would know what her brother loves too. Like trampolines," Frank added.

"When I was clinging to the tree like a scared monkey in the challenge yesterday, I heard Georgina yell for Hal to get the trampoline so George couldn't. I thought she was being stupid, because George was closer to the tramp than she or Hal was—and she'd basically just pointed it out to him," I said. "What if that's what she was trying to do?"

"George led Georgina to the peach table in a way. He got there first. I heard Georgina begging him to choose another table because he knew she loved peach," Frank told me.

"So that places him near the dish of peach slices. He had the opportunity to poison them," I answered.

"And George even said he drank toilet bowl cleaner when he was little," Frank reminded me.

"He probably wasn't trying to kill Georgina, just take her out of the competition. They both want to get legally emancipated. Only one of them can win the money. . . ."

"They've made it clear they aren't sharing," I added. "I think we need to do an evidence sweep. I call heads."

"What are we calling for?" asked Frank.

"Heads, I get to search George's stuff," I explained.

"Which means the loser has to search Georgina's," Frank said. "Which means sneaking into one of the girls' bedrooms in the middle of the night."

It's probably a good thing I lost. If Frank had to sneak into a bedroom full of sleeping girls, he might lose his lunch. And the hurling sounds would wake them all up.

I had a few butterflies myself as I softly swung open the door to Brynn, Olivia, and Georgina's room. It wasn't so bad I felt like I was going to puke them up, though.

If the cameras are on, this will probably be on the show, I thought. *Won't Mom and Aunt Trudy be proud?* I guessed I could tell them it was all part of the socioeconomic experiment. Frank and I'd given this story about how we were going to use being on the show as a project for school. It was the best explanation for why we'd be on TV with different names, pretending to be from different families. I guessed as part of the experiment one of us would have to like going through girls' personal belongings while they were asleep.

I dropped to my knees and crawled into the room. I doubted any of the girls were awake, but this way I'd be harder to spot, just in case. I crept over to Georgina's bed and slowly pulled opened the bottom drawer of her dresser. It would be stupid of her to leave any evidence in there. But it's not like Georgina was a professional.

Clothes. Of the underwear kind. That's all I've got to say about it. I searched, trying not to touch *anything*.

No evidence.

Next drawer. More clothes. Safe to touch.

No evidence.

I was out of drawers. I should check the pockets of whatever clothes she had hanging in the closet. But first, I slid the suitcase out from under her bed. Not quite empty. I felt something shift inside.

The zipper sounded as loud as machine-gun fire as I slid it open. I paused and listened. All I heard was breathing and a little snoring from somebody. Good. No one had woken up.

I lifted the lid of the case. A *Teen World* magazine. Oooh, forbidden. We'd already been deprived of all reading material. And that was it.

No evidence.

I started to slide the suitcase back under the bed.

"Don't," a girl muttered.

I froze.

"Please, don't. Don't hurt me. Please."

I recognized the voice.

"Brynn, it's me, Joe," I said softly. "I'm not going to hurt you. It's just . . . a stupid prank the other guys and I came up with."

"Don't!" Brynn cried, her voice higher.

"I'll get out right now." I stood up. "I'm going. See?" I scanned the beds until I found Brynn.

She was asleep. *She's having a nightmare*, I realized. I also realized my heart was beating like somebody was using it as a bongo. Hard and fast.

"Please," Brynn said again. Then she rolled over on her side and went silent.

Ann wasn't the only one who'd gotten freaked by what had been happening in the house. Clearly Brynn had too. Who was I kidding? The house was giving me the wiggins. The only one it wasn't bothering was the person—or people—behind all the badness.

And that's why I was in here. To get some evidence about exactly what was really going on in Deprivation House.

I crouched down and did another check under the bed. Other than the suitcase, the only thing I spotted was a pair of sneakers. Well, I wasn't necessarily looking for something big.

I had to get down on my stomach and stretch my arm out until I practically dislocated my shoulder, but I was able to get the shoes without waking up Georgina. Right shoe.

No evidence.

Left shoe.

Something. Something smooth and cool. I slid it free. Did you know they make pink Swiss Army knives? Because that's what it was. I began opening the blades. The first one was rough all down one side, and not very sharp.

It took me a second to get it. Because of the Y chromosome. It was a nail file. The next blade was regulation. I cautiously ran one finger down the flat side—and picked up a thread.

I bagged it, put the Swiss Army knife back where I found it, and crawled out of the room. Frank was waiting for me in the hall. "Let's go to the bathroom," he said.

I could tell from his face that he'd found something. "Look at this," he told me as soon as the bathroom door was safely closed behind us.

It was a baster from the kitchen. "Smell it," Frank urged.

I pulled off the squeeze top and sniffed. Something harsh and chemical. Something I suspected was the corrosive poison that had burned Georgina's tongue.

"I got something too. Off the blade of a knife I found in one of Georgina's shoes." I handed the small plastic bag to Frank.

"Looks like a piece of canvas thread," he commented. "Think it'll match the trampoline?"

"Yeah," I answered. "Think Veronica will care that her contestants are trying to kill each other?"

FRANK

11

Twisted Twins

"**W**hat am I to do about these?" Veronica tapped one crimson fingernail on her desk. The desk where the baster and the plastic bag lay.

Joe and I exchanged a glance. Wasn't it obvious what she was to do? Hand George and Georgina over to the police. Immediately.

"I wasn't trying to hurt Georgina," said George.

"That's true," Georgina jumped in. "George drank a mouthful of the same stuff, almost. His was toilet cleaner. He gave me drain cleaner. But he knew I'd be okay. And the dirt bike—I ride hard. I'm always taking spills. Wiping out isn't anything."

"It's like how Georgina knows I've taken falls off

a trampoline before," George added quickly. "She probably just thought I'd break a leg or something. Worst case."

Georgina nodded hard. "And he's always breaking stuff. He's already broken his arm twice snowboarding."

This was bizarre. Suddenly the two of them were a team.

"So you're admitting it?" Veronica asked.

Both George and Georgina's mouths dropped open. It's like neither of them had realized they had an option. Lying, for example. Something like, "I have no idea how that (fill in the blank) got in my (fill in the blank). Someone must have put it there."

"I—" George began.

"We—" Georgina started.

"So you're admitting it." Veronica cut them off. It wasn't a question this time.

"But I won't press charges!" Georgina exclaimed triumphantly. "And neither will George. So there's nothing you can do to us."

George grinned. "I would never press charges against my twin."

Veronica shook her head. "Again, I'm staggered by the knowledge a private school education provides."

"Yeah. So do we get to stay on the show? Since we aren't prosecuting each other?" George asked.

"If this gets out—and I am certainly strongly considering leaking it to the police at the earliest opportunity—it will be the district attorney who decides whether or not you will be prosecuted. And with this evidence"—again Veronica's nail tapped her desk—"I'm certain you both would be."

"Do you want money?" asked Georgina. "Call our dad. He'll give you whatever you want." She looked over at me and Joe. "You guys too. This was no big. Just me and George messing around."

"You know what I think this is?" Veronica said. "I think this is truly compelling television, which means you'll both be allowed to stay at the house."

"That's it?" I protested.

"That's it," Veronica answered. "I appreciate you boys bringing this to my attention. And I assure you, if anything like this happens again, I will personally take George and Georgina directly to the police."

She flicked her hands at us. Clearly, we were dismissed.

"I can't believe she didn't throw you out of here!" James yelled at George and Georgina as soon as we stepped out of Veronica's office. "If I had done that, I'd be in jail already."

The whole group was gathered in the hall. Staring at the twins.

"You did the drawing, too, didn't you?" Brynn demanded. "The one of the demon? And mutilated my teddy bear?"

"No way!" exclaimed George. "Georgina's the only person I wasn't sure I could beat."

"Yeah, I wanted to get George out of the running. I'm not worried about you guys," Georgina added.

One of the production assistants hurried up to the twins. "Veronica wants both of you to have a session in the Deprivation Chamber. She wants to get all your thoughts and feelings on tape—the two of you together."

"I'm next in line," James said as the three of them hurried away. "I have some things I want recorded too."

"How did you guys find out what happened so fast?" Joe asked.

Exactly what I was wondering. Joe and I had gone straight to Veronica in the morning, and she'd pulled the twins into her office while we were sitting there. No one had had time to talk to the rest of the group.

"Oh, you'll love this," Brynn answered. "They put the plasma back and told us we were getting a special treat. We were being allowed to watch TV!

And what comes on? Closed circuit of you and the psychos in Veronica's office. Of course, the camera crew was right in our faces. They wanted to get some good close-ups of our reactions."

"It really was truly compelling television," Olivia snarked.

"I think we should be asking you two how you found out what was going on with the twins so fast," James commented. He looked back and forth between me and Joe. "You guys fingered Mitch, too. You knew what was going on with him before the rest of us. What I want to know is how."

Olivia's eyes narrowed. "James is right—for once. There's something off here. You two didn't even know each other before you got to the house. How come you keep teaming up? Have you made some kind of deal? Are you teaming up to win or what?"

Olivia had alliances on the brain.

Joe laughed. I have to admit, he does a good fake laugh. Mine always sounds a little . . . fake.

"Me team up with him? The guy hates me, just because I ended up with a family who has bucks. All that garbage Mitch pulled? I thought my brother over there was behind it. I started watching him. It turned out he was just as suspicious of me."

"Yeah. I was keeping an eye on you. I didn't

like you," I said to Joe. "I still don't, just for the record."

"Anyway, we were both watching each other, and we ended up catching Mitch," Joe explained. "Then when more bad stuff started going down, I figured he"—Joe jerked his head toward me—"could probably help me figure out who was behind it. He was decent at it the last time."

"We decided to work together—just on finding out who was pulling the sabotage," I said. I turned to James. "Happy now?"

"Whatever," James muttered.

"Nice attitude," I said.

"I'm going to go get breakfast," Olivia announced. "I get headaches if I don't eat, and I want to be ready for whatever Miss Veronica decides to throw at us next."

The rest of us followed her into the dining room. The cereal bowls and silverware had already been set out by the morning's assigned cooking crew. Not that there was much actual cooking going on anymore, since we no longer had hot food privileges.

Brynn, Gail, and Hal brought in the boxes of cereal and the milk, and all they had left to do was handle the dishes. Olivia, Ann, and I were scheduled to make lunch. It would take about ten minutes to slap peanut butter and jelly sandwiches together for everyone.

"Those two really should have gotten kicked out. Who cares that they only tried to hurt each other? They cheated!" Ripley exclaimed as she shook some cereal into her bowl.

"Hang on. I thought you cared about everybody, princess," said James. His bowl was already full. You had to be fast to get food before that guy. "Isn't that your new PR image?" He grabbed the milk.

"Being nice doesn't mean you have to like everybody or that you're an idiot," Ripley exclaimed. "Are you saying I'm being mean to feel like cheaters should be thrown out of the game?"

"You're not in it to win it anyway, right?" Olivia asked. "You don't need the money. You have multiple millions, even though people are starving. And not just in other countries. Right here—"

"I get it. You hate me because I'm rich. You hate everybody who's rich. But obviously you want to be rich yourself, or you wouldn't be here trying to win a million dollars," Ripley snapped. I noticed a muscle in her neck twitch. Then she forced a smile in Olivia's general direction. "But everyone is entitled to their own opinion, right?"

"Right," said Hal softly.

I wondered if he was thinking about his opinion that sabotage was unacceptable.

"I think we should ice them out. Not deal with

them at all. They can cook for themselves, talk to themselves. I don't want to even look at either one of them," Gail said, taking the subject back to George and Georgina.

"What they do doesn't matter to me—as long as they keep doing it to each other," Brynn commented.

"But they've already done stuff to you," Olivia reminded Brynn. "That drawing of you with the monster. The teddy bear massacre."

"They said they didn't do that," Brynn told her.

"And you believed them?" exclaimed Olivia.

"George admitted he poisoned his sister and sabotaged her brakes," Brynn said. "Georgina admitted she did something that could have paralyzed her brother for life. I think if they'd gutted a stuffed animal, they would have confessed."

"Then who did do that other stuff?" asked Gail.

Was she putting on an act? Or had she and Olivia really been acting so weird about the sketchbook for some reason that had nothing to do with the investigation?

"The demon! It was the demon!" Ann shouted. She jumped to her feet so fast she knocked over her chair. "Every time one of you doubts its existence, it does something worse!"

I didn't bother asking her why a demon would

use crayon drawings and words on a wall to scare people when it was a *demon*. Logic wouldn't work on Ann. I'd finally accepted that.

"Whoever did it—including the demon," Olivia added when Ann gave her a death look, "was doing stuff before the twins even got here. Mary said she didn't put glass in the ice."

"Whatever. I'm not worried about—" James began.

Ann pointed her finger at him. "Don't say it!" Her whole arm trembled.

"Demons," James mumbled into his cereal bowl as he lifted it to drain the milk at the bottom.

"What's that?" asked Hal.

"What's what?" James answered.

"There's something stuck to the bottom of your bowl," Hal told him.

James felt around, then pulled a piece of paper off the bowl. He stared at it for a couple of seconds, then slapped it down in the middle of the table so we could all see it.

EVERYONE DIES AT DEATH HOUSE. The words were written in the same childlike handwriting as the message on the Deprivation Chamber wall and the piece of paper I'd found on the floor of the billiard room—the one that read HOUSE OF DEATH.

"That wasn't there when we set the table," Gail said.

"You looked at the bottom of each bowl?" Joe asked.

Gail frowned. "No," she admitted.

"I took the bowls out of the dish drainer," Hal told the group. "I would have seen the note then if it was there. The bowls were drying bottoms up." He stood. "I'm using the intercom to get Veronica."

"You're dropping out?" James asked. "Sweet."

"No. But I want to see the film of the kitchen and the dining room. From when I took the dishes out of the drainer until right now," Hal said.

"I want to see it too," Gail agreed.

"I'm going." Hal strode out of the room.

I studied the faces of everyone around the table, trying to decide if anyone looked nervous. Like they were about to be exposed. The thing was, everyone did look kind of nervous. Joe did. I probably did too. Nervous was getting to be the usual state for everyone in the house. Brynn was so pale even her lips had mostly drained of color. She had her eyes locked on the note.

"Hey, Ann, you'd know the answer to this. Can you see demons on film?" James asked. "Or are they like vampires?"

Ann let out a shriek of rage and hurtled out of the room.

"Just leave her alone, all right?" Joe said.

"No. It's not all right," James answered. "I don't like being told what to do by you."

It looked like another fight might be about to start up, but Hal interrupted by walking back into the dining room, followed by George and Georgina.

"Well?" Olivia asked.

"She said they weren't taping," Hal answered. "It was part of the off hours."

"Uh-uh. No way." Ripley shook her head. "Veronica would have to know we'd be talking about those two." She jerked her chin toward George and Georgina. "She'd want to get all that on film."

"Yeah. Why would she choose now to kill the cameras?" Joe asked. "There's plenty of time when we're all sitting around staring at the walls. I watch a ton of reality shows. They never leave out the part where the whole group is hating on a few people."

"You were bad-mouthing us?" George demanded.

"Ya think?" asked Gail.

"This proves Veronica and the producers did the drawing and the notes. Has to be," Olivia said. "That's why she said there was no film. The film would have shown a PA sticking that piece of paper on the cereal bowl. I'm positive. They're using the scary history of the house as part of the show."

"Half the time they lie to people about what the reality show they're on really is," Joe added. "Maybe we're in Demon House, not Deprivation House."

"If that's true, I'm suing. I'll get more than a million," said James. "Brynn, hand me the rice puffs. I'm ready for seconds."

"I guess it does make sense that Veronica is behind the drawing and note," Hal commented. "It's way too coincidental that they weren't filming at the exact time when we knew something had happened."

"Brynn! Cereal!" James commanded.

I looked over at her. She was still staring at the note. I leaned across Gail, took the cereal box that was in front of Brynn, and handed it to James. "Hey, want to go outside, Brynn? Are you finished?" I asked.

She blinked a couple of times but didn't answer.

Gail touched her arm, and Brynn gave a jerk. "Frank asked you something," Gail said. "And James issued an order, which you were right to ignore."

Brynn turned to me. "Sorry. What did you say?"

"I was just thinking if you're finished we could take a walk or something," I told her.

"Awww," James cooed.

"Sure." Brynn grabbed her light blue jacket off

the back of her chair and hurried out of the room. I followed her. We ended up sitting next to the fountain in the courtyard.

"Getting intense, huh?" I asked.

"Yeah." Her voice was flat, her eyes glassy.

"Should we make this a no demon, no murder zone?" I suggested. "No talking about any house stuff."

Brynn nodded.

I wanted to tell her right then how I felt about her. I'd been wanting to for a while. But the time never seemed right. And it still didn't. Brynn needed to chill. She was seriously stressed.

She pulled off her shoes and socks and stuck her feet in the fountain. "Get yours in here!"

"It's not exactly hot out," I said. "You're wearing your jacket." The light blue material made her hair look even blonder.

"That's the price of hanging with me. Feet in or walk your feet somewhere else."

I got my shoes and socks off fast, sat down next to her on the edge of the fountain, and plopped my feet into the water. Brynn kicked up and gave me a little splash. "I love this. This was my favorite place."

"What?" I asked.

"Oh, I was just remembering this park. When I

was little I used to go there with my mom. It had a big fountain like this. It was my favorite place," Brynn explained. "We used to splash around in it."

Her mood seemed to have completely turned around. Getting outside away from everybody for a while had been a good idea.

Brynn reached down into the fountain and flicked some water at me. Some of it landed in her blond hair and sparkled in the sun. Maybe this *was* the right time. Maybe I should tell Brynn everything I was feeling about her. . . .

Yeah, she's been feeling better for a whole minute, I thought. I decided not to say anything. Instead I splashed her back.

I woke up before daybreak the next morning and couldn't go back to sleep. I kept thinking about Brynn. My mind kept jumping back and forth between fun thoughts, like hanging out with her at the fountain, and worries. Was Brynn being specifically targeted by whoever had done that drawing and ripped up her bear?

It's not like the crayon drawing had really looked like her. The blond hair reminded me—and clearly Olivia—of Brynn. But George had thought it looked as much like his sister. And really, it was pretty generic.

I rolled over on my side and told myself to take some deep breaths and let myself drift back off. Sleep's important for a sharp mind, and I was going to need one to figure out the rest of the case with Joe.

How many people knew that bear was Brynn's?

The deep breathing didn't work. I definitely wasn't going to fall back to sleep. A run. That's what I needed. Sometimes a change of scene will give me new ideas. New angles to investigate.

I got dressed fast and headed out of my room. As I started down the main staircase, I heard footsteps behind me. I didn't think anybody else was up. I jerked my head around—and saw Joe. Wearing sneakers and sweats.

"Run?" he asked.

I nodded.

"Think Olivia and Gail will try to off you if you're seen with me?" Joe said. "We said we only teamed up to find the saboteur. We're not supposed to like hanging out together or anything."

"I'll just tell them I was trying to find a way to off you while we were jogging," I answered.

"Gotta say, I'm glad you're my brother and not George," Joe told me as we headed outside.

"Aww, that's so sweet. You prefer me to a deranged attempted murderer." I started to run. Joe matched me step for step. Neither of us likes to come in last.

"I couldn't sleep," said Joe. "I kept thinking about the notes and the drawing and the teddy bear incident. I actually believed the Twisted Twins when they said they didn't do that stuff."

"Me too. You go with the group theory that the producers are behind everything that plays on the history of the house? The old murder and the demon story?" I asked.

"Makes sense. Hal was right about the timing. It's a big coincidence that they weren't filming during the time we know that last note was put in place," Joe answered.

We left the path and entered the orchard. A few beams of light were just starting to filter through the trees. "Would that mean it was the producers who sent everybody the death threats to begin with? To get everybody scared before we even showed up?"

"We were thinking Mary had done that," Joe reminded me. "But since she's probably in a juvenile detention somewhere and the *demon* is still playing with us, I guess not. Maybe the—"

Joe grabbed my arm and yanked me to a sudden stop.

"What?" I demanded.

"Over there," he said, his voice coming out choked.

Then I saw what Joe had seen.

Brynn lying facedown in the dirt. Her light blue jacket red with blood. So much blood.

So Much Blood

"**B**rynn!" Frank shouted. I've never heard that much fear and pain in my brother's voice. Never.

We both tore over to the body. There was no way she could be alive—was there? Not with so much blood.

"She's been stabbed," Frank cried as he dropped to his knees next to Brynn.

He gently laid his fingers against Brynn's neck. Her head shifted, turning sideways. He let out a long breath.

It wasn't Brynn. It was Georgina. They had that same blond hair, and Georgina must have borrowed Brynn's jacket.

"She's alive," Frank said. "Her pulse is thready, but she's alive. I need to get a pressure bandage on her."

"You stay with Georgina," I told Frank. "I'll run back to the house and get the medic and call an ambulance." I turned and dashed off. "Cell phones," I muttered, thinking of the seconds ticking by, seconds that could save Georgina's life. "They had to take away our cell phones."

"Georgina's been stabbed!" I shouted as I pounded back into the mansion. My eyes darted back and forth as I searched for a PA. "I need somebody with phone access! We need an ambulance!"

People appeared from all directions. The stairs. The kitchen. The dining room. The front door.

"What happened?" Olivia cried.

"I don't know. All I know is she's lost a lot of blood and she needs help—now!" I answered.

"Veronica's on her way down. I'm calling an ambulance. We're tracking down the medic," a PA wearing a headset told us. "Where exactly is Georgina?"

"She's in the orchard. Back in the northeast corner. Frank's with her," I answered.

"Stabbed? As in stabbed?" asked James.

"As in clawed with demon claws." Ann clutched her charm, snapping more of the twigs.

Veronica strode into the large entryway. "Where's George?" she demanded.

I looked around. I hadn't even taken in the fact that he wasn't with the others. *Get in ATAC mode*, I told myself. I locked down everything I was feeling about what I'd just seen. I needed to be on full alert. Cool and logical and ready for whatever went down.

"I think he's in the shower," Hal said.

"I want him out and down here," Veronica ordered the PA, who began talking rapidly into her headset.

Brynn sat down on the floor. She pulled her long robe tighter around her, like she was freezing.

"I want to drop out," Gail blurted. "I want to go home. I want to go home now."

"Fine." Veronica nodded at the PA.

"You should all go," Gail told us, voice trembling. "It isn't safe here. You all know it. If you stay, you're all going to die! No amount of money is worth that."

"I'm not dying. I might kill somebody myself, but I'm not dying," James declared. He hitched up the cut-off sweats he slept in.

"I'm staying," Ripley said. "I've gotten this far."

"I'm certainly not leaving." Olivia crossed her arms over her chest.

Hal shifted from foot to foot. "I disagree that we're in danger. George is the one who—"

"Noooo!" The howl carried all the way from the second floor to the entryway. Footsteps pounded toward us, and George appeared at the top of the stairs, two PAs behind him.

He scrambled down the stairs. Barefoot. Shirtless. Dripping water. "Where is she? I want to see Georgina!" he shouted.

"Georgina is or will shortly be on her way to the hospital," Veronica told him. "And you will shortly be on your way to the police station."

"Is she okay? Is she going to be okay?" George demanded. He lunged toward Veronica, and the PAs grabbed him and jerked him back. "I want to go to the hospital with her. She'd want me to."

"I don't think having her attempted killer at her bedside would help your sister in her fight for her life," Veronica told him.

"You think I did it?" It was like it had never occurred to him. Even though Veronica had already pretty much told him the cops were coming for him.

"Ask Georgina. She'll tell you. I'd never hurt her!" George ran his hands through his wet hair.

"You tried to poison her yesterday, dude!" James exploded.

"I wasn't trying to kill her!" George shouted. "Just ask Georgina. Or let me talk to her."

"Georgina has lost a great deal of blood," Veronica told him. "She's in critical condition. She isn't able to speak to anyone."

"Critical condition? Like she could die?" asked George, all the color draining out of his face.

"You stabbed her. What do you think?" James shot back.

George's shoulders started to shake. It took me a second to realize he was crying. Sobbing. "I would never do anything to hurt Georgina," he choked out.

"You should have seen George's face," I told Frank late that night. It was the first time we'd gotten the chance to talk by ourselves. By the way, I had to sit on the edge of the tub this time. "He'd completely lost it. Crying so hard he could hardly even breathe. The police could barely get him out to the cruiser."

"Man." Frank shook his head.

"I'm not sure he did it," I said.

"I'm not either," said Frank

"Not just because of the crying . . . ," I began.

"Lots of guilty people cry," Frank agreed. "But there are still all these pieces that don't fit. I'd really like to know for sure whether the producers are behind the drawing, and the warning on the wall, and note and the bear, for one thing. It couldn't be George. He didn't have the opportunity to place the note on the cereal bowl."

"Right," I said. "Which means if it's not the producers, the person who almost killed Georgina is still in the house."

"Let's go through the list again. Who've we got?" Frank asked.

Before we could start reviewing the suspects, someone screamed.

Frank was on his feet instantly. "That sounded like Brynn!"

"Maybe a nightmare," I said as we dashed toward her room. "She was having one the other night."

It wasn't a nightmare. I knew that the instant I saw Brynn's face.

Four deep claw marks cut across her right cheek. Dripping blood.

Killer Pool

"**W**ho did it?" I burst out.

Brynn shook her head. "I don't know. I was asleep. Then I felt this ripping across my cheek."

"You didn't see anything?" Joe asked. "Or maybe hear or even smell something?"

Brynn lightly touched the scratches, then winced. "Nothing. I just . . . nothing."

"I didn't see anything either," said Olivia. She was the only roommate Brynn had left, with Georgina in the hospital.

I couldn't stop staring at Brynn's face. How had this happened? How had I let it happen? Joe and I were here to keep the other contestants safe. Now

Georgina was in the hospital and somebody had gone after Brynn.

It shouldn't have mattered that it was Brynn. I should have felt the same way if it was anyone who was supposed to be under my protection. I should have felt that way if it was James curled up on his bed, trembling, with bloody scratches on his face.

Anyway, just standing there, looking at her, feeling completely useless, was making me insane. I wanted to do *something*. Take some kind of action.

I hurried into the bathroom and wet a washcloth with warm water, then rushed back to Brynn's side. I used the cloth to wipe the blood off her cheek.

"Aww, so sweet," James said. Yeah, James was there. By the time I returned with the cloth, everybody in the group was there. No one could have slept through that terrible scream of Brynn's.

"The demon. It's getting stronger," said Ann, eyes dark and solemn. For once, she wasn't shouting. And it made her words seem less crazy and more frightening.

"Do you think there could actually be a demon?" Ripley asked. "Or maybe the house is haunted by Katrina Decter. She died here. Just two rooms over. Maybe we should ask Veronica to have somebody come in and, I don't know, do a psychic scrub-down of the place."

"Like an exorcism?" Hal asked.

"Yeah," Ripley answered. "That might help, right, Ann?"

"What do you think?" asked James. With no sarcasm. It seemed like pretty much everybody was willing to at least consider Ann's demon theory now.

I noticed Brynn's hands had blood on them too. I took one of them in mine, then used the washcloth to clean her fingers. For a second, I was hit by the fact that I was pretty much holding hands with a girl—a girl I *liked*—in front of a roomful of people. And I wasn't blushing or anything.

Maybe fear overrides embarrassment. And I was afraid, I admit it. Not of demons or ghosts. But just of the possibility that Brynn—or one of the others—could die. And that I might not be smart enough or fast enough to stop it.

"Exorcisms don't always work," Ann told the group. "This demon is strong. You finally all see that."

This wasn't good. Things were bad enough at Deprivation House without the whole group getting as demon crazy as Ann. "You know what I see?" I asked loudly. Nobody asked, "What?" but I told them anyway. "I see blood under Brynn's fingernails." I held her hand up so everyone could see. "I'm sure there's tissue under there too."

"You must have really fought back hard," Hal said. He was good at making connections. I could see him with ATAC. Unless he was the one who'd been trying to kill people. ATAC has a problem with hiring murderers.

"That's my point," I explained. "Brynn probably left her attacker with a couple of claw marks of her own. That's where the blood and tissue under her nails came from. It's ordinary blood and tissue from another human. Not some supernatural creature."

"You don't know what forms demons can take," Ann told me. "You don't have any reason to think it couldn't look like an ordinary human."

"I saw one of the old movies Nina's father directed once. The demons did all look like ordinary humans. Well, really hot ordinary humans," said Ripley.

"I didn't know he directed horror movies. Maybe that's where he came up with the idea to tell Nina her mom was possessed by a demon in the first place," Joe suggested.

"Or maybe it's because it was true!" Ann shot back. "How much more proof do you want?" She flung her hand out at Brynn. "Look at her."

"But like Frank said, we have to consider that whoever attacked Brynn left ordinary blood behind," Hal commented.

I glanced around the room. All our suspects were there, with the exception of Veronica. If one of them had attacked Brynn, they would be showing some marks too. The thing was, heat was one of our deprivations, and it got cold at night. That meant we all slept with a lot of clothes on. Everyone was wearing long pajama pants or sweats or long johns, with sweaters or sweatshirts or something else with sleeves on top. A few people— Olivia, Ann, and Hal—were even wearing gloves.

Anybody could have some wounds from Brynn's nails. Which one of them did? I had no way of knowing.

"Are you looking at me for some reason?" Joe demanded, glaring at James.

"What's your damage?" James asked.

"I saw you look at me when my brother over there was talking about how Brynn must have left some marks on her attacker." Joe took a step closer to James. "You think I did it?"

"I think you'd do anything to win. And you know a lot about how sabotage is done. I noticed that when we teamed up," I said to Joe. I thought I knew where he was going with this. And I liked it.

"Of course you'd side with him," Joe yelled at me. "You're completely prejudiced against rich people. Something bad happens, and you assume it's one of us."

"What? You think rich people are special?" Olivia demanded. "You think nobody rich would ever cheat? Or hurt somebody?"

"I know you need money a lot more than I do, Olivia," Joe shot back. "You too, James. If somebody's trying to take Brynn out of the running, I think it's a lot more likely that it's one of you."

"I don't need to take anybody out of the running," shouted James.

"Yeah? Brynn won the dirt bike race," Joe told him.

James yanked off his sweatshirt. He pulled his sweatpants up above his knees. Then he turned in a slow circle, arms stretched wide. "Anybody see any blood?" he demanded. "Anybody see any scratches from Brynn's fingernails?"

Joe had done it. He'd goaded James into showing the skin I needed to see to eliminate him. He didn't have any wounds. He couldn't have been the person who attacked Brynn.

"Your turn," James told Joe.

"Fine." Joe pulled off his sweatshirt and shoved his pajama pants up.

"It's not him," said Hal.

"Well, it's not me," I answered. I did my own strip show.

"I want to see everybody," James declared. Hal sighed and started unbuttoning his pajama top.

"I'm not showing you anything," Ripley said.

"The girls will go into the bathroom and check each other," Olivia stated. She looked over at Ripley. "Unless there's some reason you don't *want* to clear yourself."

"Fine." Ripley headed for the bathroom, followed by Olivia and Ann. I trusted them to come back with an accurate report. One good thing about all the suspicion and tension and rich-poor garbage in the group: With all the girls in the bathroom, they'd never be able to agree on some kind of cover-up.

"I'm voting for the crazy chick," James said after Hal had proved he had no scratches or blood on him.

"What about Ripley?" Hal asked. "Maybe she wanted another chance to give first aid. Maybe she's been hurting everyone for PR."

"I could see Ripley doing it too," James agreed. "And Olivia would probably eat her own foot to win."

"How would that possibly help?" Hal replied.

James ignored him. "What about you?" he asked me. "Who do you want in the Killer Pool?"

I glanced over at Brynn. She had her arms wrapped tight around her knees. Like she was afraid somebody was going to assault her again. "Let's just wait and see, okay?" I answered James. Brynn didn't need to listen to us turning what happened to her into a game.

I turned toward the door. Was the case going to be closed when the girls came back in? I could actually come up with a scenario where Ripley or Olivia attacked Brynn. They both had motives. Ripley, the good PR she'd get for coming to Brynn's aid. Olivia might have decided to take out some of the non-alliance competition.

As for Ann . . . I didn't have a motive that made sense for her. But she'd been almost hysterical for days. What was going on with her? She'd been so quiet in the beginning that Joe and I hadn't been able to get very much information out of her.

I heard footsteps in the hall. Was this it? Were we about to have absolute proof of the attacker's identity?

The door swung open. Olivia was the first one through. "We're all clean," she announced.

"I'm getting Veronica down here," I said.

"Oooh. He's calling the principal," James called.

Actually, I was calling the only suspect who hadn't been checked for wounds.

"Why drag her into it?" asked Olivia. "What if she decides to shut the show down?"

"Maybe she should," I answered. I didn't care if that happened—as long as Joe and I found the perp first. I didn't want anyone leaving the house until we had the case locked.

I hurried out to the intercom in the hall—and saw Veronica striding toward me. Clearly, she'd been alerted by a PA—or had been watching the camera footage live.

"Did you get who attacked Brynn on film?" I asked.

"We didn't start the cameras until the scream alerted us that something of interest was happening," Veronica replied.

Of interest. She had to be made of ice.

If she was the one who had attacked Brynn, it was very convenient that there was nothing on film. That was one advantage Veronica had that none of the other suspects did. She knew when the cameras were live. She controlled them.

Veronica walked past me and into Brynn's room. I rushed after her. She was as perfectly dressed and groomed as always, even this late at night. Her short lavender skirt showed a lot of her legs, but her suit jacket could be hiding the scratches Brynn had given her assailant. How were Joe and I supposed to get it off her?

An idea slammed into my head. I didn't know

if it would work, but it was worth a try. I turned around and slipped back out of the room as the rest of the group pounded Veronica with questions.

When I got downstairs to the kitchen, I went straight to the fridge and studied the contents. *Grape juice*, I decided. I poured a glass, filling it almost to the rim, then I returned to Brynn's room.

"I thought maybe you'd want something to drink," I told Brynn.

"Isn't he sweet?" James asked.

I started toward Brynn, making sure that I took a path that led me past Veronica. Then I "tripped." A second later, grape juice was splattered all over her.

Veronica let out a little shriek. "That's going to stain," Joe told her. "Give it to me and I'll run it to one of the PAs. They can do . . . whatever you're supposed to do to deal with grape juice."

She narrowed her eyes at him. "You think you're very clever, don't you?" She turned to me. "Both of you."

What was that supposed to mean? *Did* Veronica know our secret? Had she somehow managed to find out that we were ATAC?

"I know you were checking one another for wounds," she continued. "Clearly you think I might be the one who assaulted Brynn. Which is ridiculous." She slid off her jacket. The T-shirt—it probably has another name because it had lace on it—underneath showed her arms and shoulders and throat. No scratches.

"Happy?" she asked, still looking at me.

I nodded.

"I'll be charging you for the dry cleaning," she said. "Now, is there anything else?"

"What are you going to do about the demon?" Ann burst out.

"What are you going to do about what happened to Brynn?" cried Ripley. "Look what somebody did to her."

"Deprivation House is clearly bringing out the worst in one of you. At least one," Veronica answered. "It certainly affected George, and, of course, we can't allow the kind of behavior he exhibited." She gave a small shrug. "But a scratch isn't the same as a knife in the back. Any of you are welcome to leave now. Otherwise, I suggest you all start sleeping with your eyes open." She left the room without a backward glance.

"Hard-core," Joe muttered.

"I'm not going to be able to sleep at all," Brynn said. "I'm going to go to the great room and stare at the place where the TV used to be."

"I'll go with you," I immediately offered.

"I'm going to see what's in the kitchen. Maybe

there's some celery or something," said Joe. "We haven't been deprived of vegetables yet, right?"

The three of us headed out of the room. "You guys want anything? See, I can be polite to the poor," Joe added to Brynn. I could tell he was setting up an opportunity for us to talk.

"Maybe I'll get us some non–junk food," I told Brynn. She nodded. "I'd rather get it myself. I don't think my brother would be that good at serving," I added.

"What?" I said to Joe when she had disappeared into the great room. "I don't want to leave her alone."

Joe stepped close to me and lowered his voice. "Remember how we thought it was Brynn at first— in the orchard?"

"Because Georgina was wearing Brynn's coat," I answered.

"And because they have the same hair," Joe said. "I was thinking—what if someone else made the same mistake we did? What if that knife wasn't meant for Georgina? What if it was meant for Brynn?"

"And they went after her again tonight." My gut tightened just thinking about it.

"It's possible," Joe answered. "Watch her, okay? And watch yourself."

I nodded and walked into the great room. Brynn

looked so small in the huge space. "Nothing good?" she asked.

It took me a minute to realize she was talking about food. "Uh-uh," I answered. "Are you hungry?"

"No. I may never eat again. I'll have a lot of time for hobbies with the no eating or sleeping." Brynn was trying to joke around, but her voice was flat.

"So what are you going to start doing? Knitting? Field hockey? What?" I asked. I figured the best thing I could do for her was try and take her mind off the attack.

"I'm thinking . . ." Brynn's words trailed off. "My brain is gone," she admitted. "Can we just sit here? Just sit."

"Sure," I told her.

Then Brynn reached over and held my hand. I wanted to tell her that I'd never felt this way before. That she was the most amazing girl I'd ever met. But that would involve talking. And she didn't want talking. So it wasn't the time. Was it ever going to be the time?

Whoever attacked Brynn had to have been as close to her as I am right now. The thought sent a shiver through me.

She had to have screamed as soon as her face was clawed. If the attacker was so close, how did he or she get out of the room without Olivia seeing the person? If he or she was close—and they had to be—why hadn't Brynn even gotten a glimpse?

Brynn squeezed my hand. I looked down at where our fingers were twined together. I could see the dried blood under her nails.

At least she'd caused her attacker some pain. But why hadn't there been a mark on any of the suspects? Who were Joe and I forgetting?

And then it clicked. I got it. I knew who had attacked Brynn.

What I didn't understand at all was why.

JOE

14

Why Would She Do That?

"It makes sense, right?" Frank asked as he paced around the bathroom.

"Yeah. It's actually the only thing that makes sense," I told him. "It explains everything. Why neither Brynn nor Olivia got even a fast look at the attacker. Why we didn't see a mark on any of the suspects."

"It's the only thing that make sense." Frank sighed as he sat down on the edge of the tub.

"Are you okay?" I asked.

"Yeah. Why?" he replied.

"Why?" I repeated. "You know why. Because you like her. You might even love her. I wouldn't blame you if you weren't okay now that we know Brynn is behind the attack."

"I just want to understand it," Frank said. "And I don't. Not at all. Why would she do that to her own face?"

"I don't get it either. But it explains the blood under her fingernails. It was her own blood," I answered. "And nobody saw her attacker, because when Brynn screamed, there was no one in the room except Brynn and Olivia."

"What else do you think she did?" asked Frank. "Did she rip up her own bear, leave the notes, do the drawings? Did she . . ."

He couldn't finish, so I had to. "Did she do all the sabotage that's happened since Mary was taken out of the house? Did she stab Georgina?"

Frank grimaced. "Yeah. Do you think she did?"

"With this new info, anything seems possible," I admitted.

"I keep going back to the why," Frank said. "I want to understand. . . ."

"Okay, so what do we know about Brynn?" I asked.

"She likes to read. She has expensive shoes. She likes ice cream with nothing in it. . . ." Frank's voice trailed off. "It's not much. And I've spent more time talking to her than any other suspect."

"Me too. And I don't have anything good either. She made up this game where you have to come up with the best opposite for something else. And the fountain is pretty much her favorite place here."

"Yeah. She told me there was a fountain like it in this park she went to with her mom," Frank said.

Then his eyes narrowed, and I could almost see a thought ripping into his head. "What?" I asked.

"At first she said the fountain was her favorite place. Then she corrected herself and gave me the story about the park and her mom."

"Story?" I repeated. "You think it was a lie?"

"What if—and this is kind of a crazy theory—but what if Brynn was here, at the mansion, when she was a little girl? What if it's true that the fountain here was really her favorite place as a kid?" Frank asked.

"Meaning that Brynn is actually Nina?" I thought for a second. "She's the right age. Nina was four when her mother was killed. That was ten years ago. Brynn's fifteen."

"And she knew exactly where a light switch in the library was. It was so low, she shouldn't even have noticed it," said Frank. "The library used to be Nina's room."

"So why is she here? With a fake name and everything?" I'm usually pretty good at motives, but nothing about this was making sense.

"I get why she wouldn't want everyone to know

she was Nina," Frank answered. "But I don't know why she'd ever want to come back here. Every night we all hang out in the room where her mother was killed."

"Maybe that's why she's always going out to the balcony and looking down at the fountain," I suggested. "Maybe she can't stand being in that room. But then we're back to the question of why she came here in the first place."

"To stop the show from getting on TV?" Frank said. "Maybe she thought the show would bring attention back to the murder, and she didn't want that. After ten years, it's not something anyone talks about much. But with the show, that could change."

"Do you think Brynn would stab someone to shut down the show? Are we saying that she tried to kill Georgina?" The thought of Brynn doing that made my stomach do a slow roll. How must Frank be feeling? He was in love with her. And he's not like me. I fall half in love with half the girls I see. Frank's not that way.

"I hope not," Frank admitted. "But I can't let that get in the way of finding out the truth. And the truth is, she could have attacked Georgina."

"George is still a possibility," I said. "We know for sure that George poisoned Georgina and sabotaged the brakes of her dirt bike. He admitted it."

"And Georgina admitted that she sabotaged the trampoline," Frank agreed. "Let's think about the timing of the other events. Could Brynn have been behind them?"

"She definitely could have torn up her teddy bear. She could have done it, then screamed like she'd just discovered it," I answered.

Frank gave a sharp nod. "Right. All the rest of us were still in the library, talking about the crayon drawing of the girl and the demon, when she 'found' the bear. She definitely had time to set it up, then yell for us."

"Brynn left during the conversation we were having about the murder after the dirt bike race," he added. "She had the opportunity to do the drawing then. Or she could have done it earlier—in the middle of the night."

"Now that we're talking about it, I can think of other times when Brynn left the room when the rest of us started talking about Nina's murder or the demon story Nina's dad had come up with to explain things to his daughter. To Brynn, if our theory is right."

"And a lot of times, after one of those conversations, something bad would happen. The bear. The drawing," Frank said. "Maybe hearing people talk about what happened when she was little sets Brynn off."

"Maybe," I agreed. "So I think what we have to do is set her off again."

"Right. Set her off again. She'll leave—but this time we'll follow her."

The Knife

Brynn and I sat in the great room late the next night. She couldn't sleep again. Joe and I had counted on that in our plan.

My part of the plan was to stir things up by talking about the murder of the woman who might be Brynn's mom. When she bolted—which we were pretty sure she would—Joe was in place to see where she went. Right now, he was positioned out of sight in the library. He had a small mirror that allowed him to keep watch on the hallway.

So go on, I told myself. There was no point in waiting.

I opened my mouth, but I couldn't do it. I couldn't intentionally try to freak Brynn out.

I was letting my emotions get in the way. That had never happened before. Because I'd never felt about another suspect the way I did about Brynn.

Maybe I should have agreed to let Joe do this part. He'd offered. But I was the natural one to offer to sit up with Brynn. She and Joe were friends, yeah. But he hadn't spent most of last night holding her hand. The way I was holding her hand right now.

Do it, I ordered myself. *It's the plan. If she's the perp, you have to know it. You can't put everyone in this house at risk because you won't step up.*

I swallowed hard. My mouth and throat were as dry as if I'd been eating sand. "Sometimes when it's really quiet in here, like now, I start thinking about the murder," I said, my voice coming out rough. "I've never been in a room where somebody was killed before. At least not that I know of."

"Me either," Brynn said. Her fingers tightened on mine. They were cold. And trembling a little.

"Do you think it's true that emotions can get trapped in a place? I saw something like that on this show, *Spectral*." The only reason I'd ever watched it was because Joe was addicted—even though the ghosts on the show were so clearly fake. "People who are sensitives are supposed to be able to feel the fear and anger that's trapped wherever something violent has happened."

"You're starting to sound like Ann," Brynn told me. She pulled her hand away. Was she getting ready to take off?

Not yet. I had to push harder.

"I'm not talking about demons," I answered. "I'm just talking about psychic energy. A man killing his own wife in front of their daughter—that's intense stuff. Maybe it does leave some kind of residue. Maybe it's my imagination, but when the room is almost empty, I think I can feel something."

Brynn jerked to her feet. "I think . . . I'm going to go to bed."

"You sure?" I asked.

She didn't answer. Just left. The way she always seemed to leave when the murder came up.

I forced myself to do a slow twenty-five count. Then I stepped into the hall. Joe was waiting for me.

"Did she go into her room?" I whispered.

He shook his head. "Down the stairs."

That's not what I wanted to hear. *What you want is the truth,* I reminded myself.

"Come on," said Joe. Keeping in the shadows, we crept over to the head of the stairs. Just in time to see Brynn heading out the front door.

Joe and I rushed down the stairs. I strode over to the dining room window and peered outside. "She's in the garden. She's walking fast, " I told Joe.

We let her get a little more of a head start, then followed. Through the garden and into the orchard. The orchard where Georgina almost died.

Why was Brynn out here?

She started to run. She stumbled over a root but didn't slow down. Not until she got to the northeast corner. Then she dropped to her knees and began to dig. Only about twenty-five feet from where Georgina's blood had soaked into the ground.

Joe and I froze. Watching.

What was she doing?

She clawed at the ground. Frantic. I could hear her ragged breathing as she pulled something free. Something that glinted in the moonlight. It took me a second to register what it was.

A knife.

Brynn stood up and raised the blade high in the air. Aimed at her chest.

"No!" I screamed. "Brynn, stop!"

"Don't!" Joe shouted.

Brynn started to bring the knife down. I launched myself at her. I hit the back of her knees with my shoulder, and we both hit the ground.

Where was the knife? Did she still have it? I didn't see it in her hand.

"Got it!" Joe cried.

"Brynn, what were you doing?" I exclaimed. I grabbed her by the shoulders and stared into her face. "What were you trying to do?"

Her eyes were blank. I don't think she saw me at all.

I gave her a light shake. "Brynn!"

She didn't answer. She didn't even blink. It was like I was holding a dead body.

JOE
16

Game Over

"It's over." Ripley set her suitcase down in the entry hall.

"I don't see why the show's canceled," James complained aloud. "We know Brynn was the psycho."

"This time," said Hal. "Maybe they figured three people trying to end the game meant it really shouldn't happen."

"If we want to keep going, they should let us," Olivia declared.

"Georgina did almost die. And Mitch killed a PA," Hal reminded us. "Maybe the show should have been shut down a long time ago."

Olivia raised her eyebrows. It was like even now

157

she couldn't believe Hal was disagreeing with her in front of everyone.

"The taxis should be here shortly," Veronica announced as she joined us.

"I think we should each get some cash," James told her. "The next person to drop out would have gotten paid. And we're being forced to drop out."

"Yeah, we should get something," Olivia agreed.

"You've all been given something very valuable," Veronica told us.

"What? I wasn't given anything," James protested.

"You were all given the chance to realize that you have more than you need. Every one of you. You've learned that you can get by with much less than you ever thought," Veronica explained. I could tell she was trying not to smile.

"Maybe we've all been given the chance to sue you and the other producers," Olivia shot back.

"You all signed releases when you agreed to be on the show," Veronica reminded us. "You agreed not to hold the producers responsible for any injuries. And it was made clear that the show could be stopped at any time, and that it might not even air at all."

"Hey, Bobby T said the option on his blog has been renewed. He's getting a boatload of cash,"

Ripley announced, reading a text message on her phone. We'd gotten all our luxury items back an hour ago.

"He has a boatload of debt, too," James said. "The loser probably didn't break even."

I heard a car pull up in front. Then two more. It was time to go home.

Olivia suddenly rushed over to us. Make that Olivia suddenly rushed over to Frank.

"Here." She thrust a large sheet of paper into my brother's hands. "I know Gail would want you to have this—even though she practically gave birth to a cow the day you almost caught her sketching it."

Frank and I exchanged a quick glance. So that was why the girls had acted so freaky that day. They were trying to keep Frank from seeing the sketch book, but not for any crime-related reason.

I turned my attention to the sketch. It was the worst drawing of Frank you could possibly imagine. The eyelashes on him. Step back. It was like he was the spokesboy for a new kind of man mascara or something.

I started to snicker. Then it hit me. Olivia wasn't handing over a sketch of *me*.

I smiled as something else hit me. Gail probably took the sketch she did of your hero home with her. She was probably sleeping with it under her pillow.

Yeah. She'd wanted to keep the one she'd drawn of me. I'm pretty sure that's what the deal was. And I'm a detective, so I should know.

One of the cab drivers gave an impatient honk.

"I guess we'd better get going," Olivia said. "Sorry if I got a little intense sometimes," she added to Frank.

"Everybody did," Frank answered.

"I just wish we'd realized what was going on with Brynn earlier," Frank said quietly as we stowed our suitcases in the trunk of the second taxi. "Maybe we could have helped her."

"She's getting help now," I reminded him. "The psychiatric hospital is where she belongs."

Frank nodded, but I knew he was still running through scenarios where we were able to stop Brynn before she hurt anyone.

"Let it go, Frank," I told him as we got into the taxi together. "We completed our mission. None of the contestants ended up dead."

He nodded again. But he was still thinking about her. I wasn't sure if he'd ever stop.

FRANK

"I've got to do it," I told Joe. "But you don't have to come. It's not an official mission."

"Are you kidding?" Joe said. "I'm not passing

up the chance to wear my Diesels." He patted the jacket pocket where he'd stashed the sunglasses that had been part of his Joe Carr cover. He hadn't been able to wear them since we came back from Deprivation House a few months ago. There would have been *waaay* too many questions. Our parents are generous and everything. But they'd never shell out for three-hundred-dollar shades. And it's not like Joe has that kind of cash.

We mounted up on our motorcycles. Four hours later, we rode through the wrought-iron gates of Plainview Hospital. It was supposed to be the best in the country. It looked like a nice place. There were some patients sitting in the front garden, getting some sun. But it was still hard to think of Brynn here.

"You ready?" Joe asked after we parked.

I wasn't. But more time wasn't going to change that. "Yeah," I told him. I led the way inside and gave our names—our cover-story names—to the woman at the front desk. "Nina's doctor will take you back," she said. "She wants to talk to you before you see Nina."

Was Brynn—I still thought of her as Brynn—okay? She'd been in here for a couple of months. Had her doctor been able to help her at all? Would she be happy to see me? And Joe? Or would we just be part of a horrible memory?

"Hi, I'm Dr. Bastajian." A short woman with a ponytail walked over and shook our hands.

"How is Brynn—I mean Nina?" I asked in a rush.

"She's making progress," the doctor answered. "But she still has a long way to go. She's just beginning to remember what happened when she was back in the house."

"She blanked everything out? Trying to stab herself? Stabbing Georgina?" Joe asked.

"It's more complicated than that. Being back in the house where she saw her mother killed by her father was extremely traumatic. Nina began to dissociate, have blackouts."

"So she wasn't even aware she was doing things like putting pieces of glass in with the ice cubes?" I asked. We'd figured out that that's when Brynn had started breaking down. Mary had insisted she hadn't been responsible for the glass that cut up James's mouth as well as the fire in Bobby T's room and the knives in Brynn's makeup bag, and it turned out she was telling the truth. Mary had been doing a lot of sabotage—but nothing violent. Sending us e-mail death threats was more her style. But Brynn . . . She'd even done things to hurt *herself*!

"She absolutely wasn't aware," Dr. Bastajian said.

"I think in some way, she was trying to make the demon story that her father told her true. It was too horrific to accept that her father had simply killed her mother."

"So the demon story . . . ," said Joe. "I mean, I know it wasn't true, but are you saying that Brynn's mother didn't actually try to attack her?"

"No. Nina was beginning to remember what really happened that night," Dr. Bastajian explained. "Her mother hadn't started using drugs or alcohol again. But she had decided she wanted to leave her husband. They fought, and he killed her."

"And he came up with that story about the demon and convinced Brynn—Nina—that that was what happened," I said.

"Exactly," the doctor agreed. "Nina grew up with her grandparents in Indiana, living a quiet life away from all of this. Her grandparents helped her change her first and last name to Brynn Fulgham, so that she would be safe from nosy media hounds. Then, when Nina realized a reality show was going to be filmed in her old house, the house where the murder happened, she was determined to go back. She thought being there would somehow allow her to remember everything that really happened that night. The pieces she was starting to remember were haunting her."

"So are we supposed to not mention the old murder or the stuff Brynn did when she was having one of her episodes?" Joe asked.

"Just follow her lead. Don't push. But if she wants to talk, it's fine," Dr. Bastajian said. "Come on. I'll take you to her room." She led us through a maze of hallways, then tapped on a closed door. "Nina, you have visitors." She swung the door open.

And I saw Brynn. For the first time in months. She sat in front of a small desk in the corner of her room. And she looked . . . she looked like Brynn. Clear-eyed. A little smile on her face. "Hi," she said, without quite looking at me or Joe.

"Hey, Nina," said Joe. I guess he could tell I was having trouble getting words out.

"You can keep calling me Brynn," she said.

"So, uh, how are you?" I asked. It was like I had just learned English a few days ago. It was hard to find any words.

Brynn lifted her hands, then let them fall in her lap in a helpless gesture. "Let's talk about you guys instead. So I guess being in the house was good for you two at least."

Joe and I glanced at each other.

"I mean, you two, you got to know each other. And you're here, together. So I guess you finally kind of became friends," Brynn explained.

"Yeah, I guess we finally kind of did. Getting winning or losing out of the picture helped," Joe told her.

Dr. Bastajian's cell beeped. She scanned the text message. "Nina, your father is here. I'm assuming—"

"I don't want to see him," Brynn answered, her voice hard.

The doctor nodded. "I'll go speak to him. Enjoy your visit."

"I can't believe he thinks I'd want to see his face!" Brynn burst out. "Now that I know what he did. And he'll never have to go to prison for it. He's already had his trial. He can't be tried again for the same crime. And it's my fault. It was my testimony that got him off."

"You were a little girl. You believed what your father told you," I said. "Pretty much anyone would."

"I just hate that he gets to live his whole life as this man who killed his wife to protect his daughter. No one will ever know the truth." Brynn took a deep breath. "Sorry," she said. "I know I'm going off. I'm working on dealing with it. And dealing with what I did too. I wrote to Georgina. I tried to explain. She was actually really great about it."

"Did you hear the movie option on Bobby T's

blog got renewed?" Joe asked. "It's getting an insane number of hits a day."

I guess Joe was having trouble knowing what to say too. He was kind of babbling.

"If I wanted to get info out there, Bobby T's blog is where I'd want it," Joe continued.

He wasn't babbling. "I'm sure Bobby T would be happy to put the real story about your dad on his site. At least then people would know the truth," I told Brynn.

"You think he'd do that?" asked Brynn.

"Are you serious?" Joe replied. "He'll have it on there today if you want."

"I want," Brynn said. "I want to tell what I did too. I want to try to explain. Apologize."

"You weren't even aware of what you were doing," I reminded her.

"I still did it," Brynn told me. "I have to take responsibility. I'm not going to be like my father. I'm not going to try to come up with a story that makes me a hero. Or that just makes what I did seem okay somehow."

She was an amazing person. No wonder she was the first girl I fell in love with.

But I'd never be able to see her again. Frank Dooley didn't really exist. I'd only been able to be him for a couple more hours. To say good-bye.

"Are you okay?" Joe asked me when we left.

"Yeah. What about you? Are you going to be okay?" I climbed on my bike.

"Me? Yeah," said Joe.

"Are you sure? You know you're not going to be able to wear the Diesels again," I reminded him.

Joe grinned. "Even without them, I'm still the more happenin' Hardy. And someday a girl is going to realize that absolute truth!"